Summer

of

L.U.C.K.

Summer

of

L.U.C.K.

BY

LAURA SEGAL STEGMAN

INtense Publications
www.intensepublications.com

INtense Publications

Paperback ISBN-13: 978-1-947796-56-0

Summer of L.U.C.K.

Copyright © 2020 Laura Segal Stegman

This edition published by arrangement with INtense Publications LLC. The opinions expressed by the author are not necessarily those of INtense Publications LLC.

www.INtensePublications.com

Printed in U.S.A

＊

Summer of L.U.C.K. is dedicated to Hugh
Stegman, the love of my life; to Susan Segal, whose
support for this project never wavered; and to Claire
and Bro Segal, who taught me to love reading.

＊

Table of Contents

Chapter One

JUNE 12

The scrape of a sliding door sent eleven-year-old Darby McAllister diving back into the swimming pool. Underwater, her mom's scolding couldn't touch her. She held her breath for as long as possible, but once she came up for air, the voice from the second story deck delivered its predictable reprimand.

"Darby, I already told you to get ready for riding. Out of the pool *now*."

"Oh, M-M-..." Darby stopped short. She gave it another shot, hoping Mom hadn't heard her stutter. "I'd rather s-s-swim." Squeezing her eyes shut, she waited for the response to land like a blow, the way it usually did. Would it hurt as much as the muffled laughter from new students had yesterday when she'd stumbled over reciting her riding academy's safety rules?

"Aren't you listening?" Her mother's volume rose. "And *speak slowly*!" The door banged shut.

Scrambling out of the water, Darby stuck out her tongue in her mom's general direction. She ran a towel over her reddish-brown curls and drifted into the house through her dad's open studio door.

"Hi sweetie," he said.

She kissed his head then hung across his chair as he rubbed an eraser over the foot of a dancing female figure on his sketchpad.

"One more day before you leave for camp," he added with a wink, flicking off a few droplets that fell from her hair onto his shoulder.

Darby brightened. Last summer, her buddy Monica never, ever made fun of her stutter. No one had even mentioned it. And she rode Camp Inch's horses for fun, the way it used to be before trophies mattered. *To Mom anyway.*

She sprinted upstairs to change, relieved that the smells emanating from the kitchen meant they'd be eating home tonight. The memory of last night's misery at the restaurant still stung.

After the third time her mom had asked, "Have you decided?" Darby lowered her head, convinced everyone in the place must be looking their way. Frozen with uncertainty, she could have sworn she heard a foot tapping under the table. The second she closed the menu; her mother waved a finger at the server.

"Sir!"

"Hang on, Marcia." Dad patted Darby's hand. "He's coming."

The server smiled. "You all set?"

"Y-Y-yes," Darby's eyes had darted toward her mother, anticipating the grimace. "I-I-I." With everyone's stares drying up her words, she finally pointed to the burger combo.

The server took the menu. "You got it, kiddo. Be right up."

"Honey, you want something to drink?" her dad asked.

Darby shook her head, tightening her lips. *Better to shut up than stutter again.*

"Have you been practicing your breathing?" her mother demanded. Without waiting for a reply, she turned with a frown to the business chart beside her plate. "You'll need sharp communication skills to get anywhere."

Another warning. If I stutter, I'll never be successful like my parents. Queasy with mortification, Darby had left most of her meal untouched.

Now, she sat beside her camp suitcase, fiddling with her blazer. *Maybe today's my lucky day, and no one at the riding academy will talk to me.* She reached into the suitcase to check under the outfits her mom chose, making sure her butterfly net hadn't been discovered. *Nope, still there.* Her eyes sparkled at the inclusion of one thing her mother hadn't authorized.

As she smoothed the clothes back into place, something sweet, like the chocolate milk she couldn't manage to order last night, lingered in the air. *What's that smell?*

Four weeks had passed since the last time Justin Pennington uttered a word.

Not that he didn't have plenty to say. But he had his reasons for clamming up.

On the Saturday before summer camp, Justin surveyed the piano keys. He ran a few scales, trying to avoid turning his head toward his dad's picture atop the polished lid. *No use.* He shoved the piano bench backwards. A lump filled his throat, and his insides ached with deepening gloom.

He headed to the bay window's seat and hurled his stocky frame onto its cushion. Despite the bright Milwaukee sun outside, his expression darkened. He pulled the curtains closed around himself, wiped his wet face with the soft material, and glared out the window.

On the lawn, a baseball glove lay exactly where he'd left it after his twelfth birthday last Sunday. He covered his solitary reflection in the window with one hand and tugged at a handful of his sandy hair with the other, unsure if the leaden weight in his stomach would ever go away. As he calculated the prospect of eight weeks at Camp Inch being any better than home, he shut his eyes. *It can't be worse.*

Justin bolted upright at the sight of his mom pulling into the driveway. Sunlight on the silver hood of his Dad's sedan, which had been dull with dust when she'd left a few hours ago, glinted off its now shiny finish.

Why couldn't she have left it the way it was? He backed away from the window, ignoring her wave. Swallowing hard, he realized the dirt covering the car had been the last connection he'd had. Now it was gone too, just like his dad.

Justin hastily wiped his fingerprints from the pane with a corner of the curtain. A sweet aroma turned him toward the kitchen. *Cake? No, she hasn't baked since...* He sniffed again. *Smells like cotton candy at the Little League snack bar.* But then it vanished.

"Justin," called Mom. Startled, he rushed over to the piano. By the time she entered the room, he appeared busy flipping through music books.

"Hi dear, sorry it took longer than I thought." She opened her carryall. "I finally picked up some wallpaper samples for the O'Hara's and stopped to show them. You okay?"

Without looking up from the sheet music, Justin nodded.

"Would you like to see?" she began, absorbed in the swatches. Before he had a chance to respond, as if he would have, she left. Seconds later, she came back. "Remember, you need to finish packing your things." When he didn't move, she added, "Camp starts Monday. Would you, uh, would you like some help?"

Justin stayed silent, carefully returning the books to the

music rest, and glanced up. For a moment, they stared at each other. Then she turned away, but not before he glimpsed her eyes reddening with tears.

Less than one hundred miles away, in a Wisconsin suburb, an olive-skinned boy practiced before his bedroom dresser mirror. "My name is Naz. My name is *Naz*," he repeated. "*My* name is Naz. My *name* is Naz. I have ten years... I *am* ten years old." He made a face at his unsteady English. *I hope kids at Camp Inch understand me. Probably no one will speak Arabic like I do -- or even French.*

The beauty of Mamá's music drew him to the door. "*Vissi d'arte, vissi d'amore*," she sang, "*non feci mai male ad anima viva!*" Although she hadn't spotted him, she seemed to know he was there. "Are you practicing, precious?" she said, using English.

Naz scooted back to the mirror. "I am in Mil-wau-kee," he said, hesitating over the name of his new town. It hadn't quite settled in his brain, just as he and Mamá hadn't quite settled in their new house.

Moving aside two boxes, he gazed out his window, hoping for something there that would remind him of home in Morocco. "Lake Mich-ig-an," he pronounced slowly. The water stretching to the horizon appeared grayer than the perfectly blue Mediterranean Sea on his country's coast.

He went to the dresser and pulled open his beloved album, a parting gift from Papá, to search for a letter tucked between pages of family photos. By now, he'd practically memorized it.

… I will miss you both deeply, but Mamá's good fortune to perform with a symphony is very important to her, Papá wrote in Arabic. While we are apart, I encourage you to continue improving your English and embrace this opportunity to explore a new part of the world…

Naz replaced the letter and hugged the album to his chest, rubbing away tears that came down his cheeks too quickly to stop them from striking the leather. He grabbed a few colorfully wrapped Doux Rêves taffy candies from a box on the dresser and sorted through the flavors. Finally, he tossed a coconut piece, Papá's favorite, into his mouth.

Flopping down on the bed, so much smaller than the one he'd left in Morocco, he remembered Papá's pledge to buy him a new bicycle when he and Mamá return from America. *If we return. What if she decides her "good fortune" is more "important" than going home?*

A sugary smell hit him. *Did I drop a Doux Rêves onto the bed?* He pulled back the covers. Nothing there.

"*Mon chéri,*" called Mamá. "*Viens, allons au dîner.*" She laughed, translating her words from French to English. "Let's go to dinner. Do you understand?"

Naz, his mood lifting, ran downstairs to her warm embrace.

Far away, inside a seemingly abandoned warehouse near Michigan's Camp Inch, a dusty carousel calliope creaked slowly back to life.

Chapter Two

JUNE 14

Naz emerged from a long black car into Camp Inch's parking area, tingling with expectations that hadn't gripped him since well before he'd hugged Papá goodbye. He spun around, gaping at all the automobiles, their trunks popping up and doors slamming shut. His gaze followed a never-ending procession of electric carts threading in and out. The young drivers, whose caps matched their bright yellow CAMP INCH STAFF T-shirts, busied themselves loading luggage, or campers, or sometimes both, then zipped off.

While Mamá opened the trunk, Naz ran to a field of grass with a sign containing two words: GREAT LAWN. He rolled over and over and over again on the greenery, inhaling its fresh-mowed smell. Compared with Morocco's deserts, the surrounding hills, towering trees, spacious grounds, and blossoming flowers looked unlike any landscape he'd ever seen. Catching his first glimpse of a two-story wooden structure before him, he jumped in delight.

"Mamá!" he called, pointing at its sharply angled roof and four unusually large round upstairs windows framed by a decorative balcony.

She joined him, her heels sinking into the lush lawn. "*Oui, mon chéri*, Branch Hall is even more beautiful than the photograph!"

As they started up one of the four broad corner stairways, Naz took hold of the grapefruit-size wood globe topping a post, nearly able to swing from it. He ran to one of the wicker chairs, as white as the building itself, that dotted its covered veranda. Rocking back and forth, he pleaded, "Sit beside me, Mamá."

"I would love to, but we must return to get your cabin assignment."

Naz followed her to the parking lot, walking backwards to enjoy all the pinks, yellows, violets, oranges, and reds that ran through abundant flower beds planted between the stairways.

Nearby, Darby hoisted herself onto the running board of her dad's SUV. Shielding her eyes from the warm June sun, she scanned the overflowing crowd in search of Monica, her bunkmate from last summer. "There!" she whispered to her father, and a dark-haired girl rushed up.

"How many feathers?" teased Monica, as if it were yesterday when they'd counted every single one they'd collected after their raucous pillow fight.

"One thousand four hundred seventy-eight." Darby threw back her head with laughter, barely noticing the surprised glance her parents exchanged at the sound of her making so much noise.

"What cabin are you? I got Six South."

"I don't kn-kn-know yet." But just then, a cart with a CAMP REGISTRAR sign rolled up. The driver took her name, marked it on his clipboard, and handed Darby's father a cabin envelope. She grabbed his arm, almost shaking it, until he flipped it over. "Six South!"

The girls slapped high fives, and Monica dashed off. "See you there."

"Don't scratch that," Darby's mother warned the two staffers who were collecting the luggage. She leaned down for a quick kiss from Darby then got into the McAllister SUV, issuing one final instruction through the window. "Make us proud, dear."

"All right, M-m-mom. I'll be g-g-good." Darby cringed at her mother's frown, but her father's bear hug restored her spirits. He helped her into the rear of the Registrar's eight-passenger cart behind a row stacked with her trunk and other gear. They took off, and she twisted to wave out the back.

"Have a ball!" Dad called with a grin.

Darby hugged her knees to her chest as the driver navigated around the parking area, picturing the summer ahead as Monica's bunkmate. *I can't wait to see which one she picks for us. With a best friend like her, maybe speaking perfectly isn't important. No matter what Mom thinks.*

When the cart stopped between a silver sedan and a long black car, she noticed two boys and two women, probably their moms, waiting for cabin assignments. One of the kids, whose olive skin matched his khaki shorts, had just stuck out his hand to the older, sandy-haired, stocky boy. "My name is..." he was saying.

Darby bent slightly closer. *What'd he say? Was it Naz? Or maybe Nat?*

The stocky boy stared back silently. He kept his hands in his pockets.

Isn't he going to say anything? Darby sat upright, bumping her head on the cart's rear railing. "Ow!" she exclaimed so loudly that the two boys turned her way.

Everything slowed down. Just as curiously, calliope music, like the rolling kind on a carousel, filled her head. Darby saw both boys peer around. *They heard it too.* The younger kid smiled at her. The older one looked away, his face unreadable.

The two women kept chatting with the Registrar, and around them, other conversations continued, as if nobody else had noticed.

Darby kept her gaze on the two boys. *Where's it coming from?* It appeared as though they actually shrugged in response.

Her eyes widened. *I didn't say anything out loud. Did I?*

After the Registrar assigned the olive-skinned kid to One North and the stocky one to Eight North, Darby tried not to stare as they said their goodbyes. Naz – or Nat – clung to his mom for a long hug, her blondness contrasting with his black hair. Then he hopped into the cart two rows ahead of Darby. The older boy almost rushed into the front seat. *He acts like he's in a hurry to get rid of his mom. Kind of like me.* She bit back a giggle.

When the cart moved ahead, Darby clutched the rail, trying to see around or above the luggage. *Should I ask Naz-or-Nat about the weird music?* Meanwhile, several other boys got on. The kid told them his name – this time she confirmed it as Naz -- and they struck up a conversation.

The summer breeze ruffled her hair as they drove past the Great Lawn toward a tree-ringed plaza. Relief that she didn't have to speak to anyone loosened her hold on the rail, and Darby leaned back, daydreaming about last year's plan, which she intended to carry out this summer. *With Operation L.U.C.K., Monica and I won't need pillow fights for good times!*

⚬

The Registrar stopped at the NORTH CIRCLE marker. Justin watched as the other boys, pals already, jumped out. One camper, his black hair darker than that of the kid who had wanted to shake Justin's hand, shouted, "Let's race," and they took off.

He wandered slowly into North Circle. By now, he was sort of used to being alone. And not talking. *But that strange music threw me. I almost said something.* Justin trembled at the idea of ending his long silence, unsure whether the prospect triggered distress... or comfort. Bits of conversation from inside cabins ringing the perimeter caught his ear, and his resolve returned. *Nothing's changed. I don't have much to tell anyone. And besides, there's no one I want to talk to.*

After passing One, Two and Three North, Justin took a shortcut to Eight North through a long building in the center with more bathroom stalls, showers, and sinks than he'd ever seen in one place. In the mirror, he tried tugging at his hair, which ordinarily helped clear his head. But last weekend's visit to the barber made that impossible. He stared at his reflection. *Will it ever grow back?*

Behind him, the wall calendar said JUNE 1999. *Six months left until the year 2000.* Justin and his dad had been excited at the prospect of witnessing the turn of a new century, but now he couldn't care less. He moved his finger over the grid's squares to today's date. FLAG DAY HOLIDAY. With nothing to celebrate, he made his way out through the opposite door.

Eight North, built like the other seven cabins of golden

wood, sported a slanted, forest-green roof whose color reminded Justin of the flat eaves from his old Lincoln Logs set. After confirming his stuff had arrived into the pile of luggage, he left his footlocker, took his duffel bag, went up the steps, and poked his head inside.

Justin warmed to the room's fresh pine smell as he surveyed the six sturdy bunk beds. Two stood against each long wall, with the ones on the sides paired with windows that bathed the space in light.

Unnoticed by a pair of counselors delivering a trunk to some kids on the left, Justin veered to a vacant bunk on the right. Tossing his duffel bag onto the deep-blue blanket as the counselors headed to the door, he climbed up and peered through the window with an uncomfortably familiar sense of being invisible.

Outside, one of the counselors asked the other, "Whose trunk is this?"

"Justin Pennington hasn't checked in, must be his." Though they lowered their voices, Justin heard him add, "The one who lost his father in April."

He shut his eyes.

"Poor kid." Opening the door, the taller counselor did a double take. "Oh, hey, Justin, there you are. I'm Franklin, and this is Ben. Welcome to Eight North, buddy. Are you all set up?"

Justin nodded but stayed put while they hauled in his footlocker, his eyes on a cabin mate pulling a fancy flashlight from his suitcase.

"Hey guys, check this out," said the flashlight boy. "It has a key ring, ruler, and mini wrench, besides a bunch of other stuff."

When the others gathered around, Justin longed to join them. *But what would I say?* It didn't seem right to point out that if you put the counselors' first names together, it made Ben Franklin. Or that the Founding Father was one of his favorite historical figures. *They probably wouldn't care about that.* His mom hadn't when he'd brought it up a few months ago.

Carousel calliope music from outside turned him toward the window. *What IS that?* An olive-skinned camper's face appeared in a matching window next door. A voice said, "I am pleased to see you." *It's the kid from before. Is it in my head? Can't be -- it sounds just like him.* Justin twisted around. *Doesn't anyone else hear it? Or the music?* But his cabin mates remained absorbed in the flashlight's wonders. Justin turned back to the window and returned the kid's smile. *What did he say his name was?*

The counselors announced dinner, so Justin filtered outside with the others, and Hugh, the boy with the fancy flashlight, took him in tow. "It even works underwater!" he boasted.

Justin nodded vaguely then glanced toward the cabin next door as they left. He tilted his head to listen, but no music sounded, and nobody showed up in the window. *I couldn't have imagined that, right?* He hoped not.

Inside One North, Naz gazed around, looking for a loudspeaker that would explain the funny music and finding nothing but a cabin full of kids. But that was enough. He settled back on the top bunk he'd secured, with its great view. Drawers provided exactly the right space for his clothes. He knew some of his cabin mates' names already, including bunkmate Brough, who had to spell his name twice so Naz could remember it, and Charlie, Odell, and Ryan from the cart ride.

Even Counselor Woody matched perfectly. "*Bonjour, mon ami,*" Woody had greeted him, explaining he grew up in a place called Quebec where everyone spoke French, just like Naz, as well as English. Naz tried to picture his own hair like the counselor's, which ended in tangles below his shoulders, but he doubted Papá would ever allow it.

Brough tossed up a nerf ball. Naz caught it and threw it to Charlie. After everyone joined in, their commotion raised the noise level considerably.

The cabin's other counselor arrived, glowering. "Let's get organized here," he said, lifting a whistle close to his lips. The room fell silent, making his raised voice sound even louder. "Mealtime. Let's go!" Addressing Naz, he added, "WE… GO… NOW…"

Naz stopped in his tracks.

As the others filed out, Woody whispered to Naz in French. "Don't worry, Rich is just an impatient guy. Come on, let's eat."

After the Registrar dropped Darby at a path leading to a SOUTH CIRCLE sign, she sprinted to Six South. Inside, a young woman in a CAMP INCH STAFF T-shirt said, "Hi, I'm Sally. And you're…?"

"Darby. Have you s-s-seen Monica?"

"I'm not sure who came in while I was out but go ahead and choose any bunk you want. Other than this."

Darby followed Sally's pointing finger to the window bunk by the door marked with a tennis racket above and a white sweater below. She made a beeline across the cabin to the other window bunk, admiring the bright yellow blankets that replaced last year's dark green ones, then reserved the top with her duffel bag and the bottom with her cabin envelope. *Since I picked the bunk, maybe I'll let Monica pick if she wants top or bottom.*

"Is this your first time here?" asked Sally.

"Oh no, it's my second," said Darby, relieved that the pillow-

fight hadn't been reported to this year's staff. "My friend's going
to bunk with me again."

The door opened, and Monica poked her head inside.
"There you are. I was looking all over for you."

"I already picked out our..." Darby began.

THUD! THUD! THUD!

"What's that?" Darby backed up at the vibration.

Rolling her eyes, Monica stepped out to hold the door. "It's
my friend Lindsay."

How did she get to know someone else so fast? Darby's
cheeks started burning.

Lindsay backed in, dragging a footlocker. Monica helped her
push it to the bunk by the door and tossed the white sweater
onto the top bed next to the tennis racket.

Darby fought to quell a jumpy sensation. Don't say
anything. You'll just stutter.

"Howdy," said Lindsay with a quick glance after Monica
introduced them. While other campers began filtering into the
cabin, she flipped open her footlocker and sorted through her
things.

Darby pulled Monica across the room. "I saved us a bunk
over here," she whispered.

"Oh no, I promised I'd bunk with Lindsay when I talked her
into coming to camp," Monica explained, adding hastily, "I'm

sorry."

Darby's heart sank, her dreams of bunking with the only close friend she'd ever had shattering. *But we planned it last summer. How could you forget?*

"But look, I saved the one next to us so we can both have top beds."

"No," said Darby, scratching her prickling skin. "I-I-I'll k-k-keep this bunk."

"It's so ot-hay in here," exclaimed Lindsay, winding her long blonde hair into a ponytail on her way out the door. "Let's go get some air."

"Old-hay on," Monica called.

"Old. Hay." Darby shook her head. "Why are you talking like that?"

"My granny taught us Pig Latin last week."

Monica's giggle stopped abruptly when Darby turned away. "You'll like Lindsay. I promise." She backed off and headed outside.

Darby pressed her lips together to keep from calling after her. *What about our plan to check out the orange Operation L.U.C.K. building? Did you forget that too?*

"Girls," said Sally, "almost time for the cookout. Let's get ready to go."

But Darby climbed up onto her bunk, scarcely noticing

carnival music sounds. When they got louder, she looked out the window, then inside. Everyone else simply chattered. *How come nobody but me hears it? Where's it coming from?*

She turned back to the window where the view outside revealed nothing other than a pathway between South and North Circles. *It's stopped anyway.* Darby scrunched up her face, hoping no one could see the tears stinging her cheeks.

Naz followed his counselors to dinner down a hedge-lined pathway that ran between the girls' and boys' cabins. His mouth watered with visions of what American foods he would encounter at his first camp cookout.

With a whistle blast for emphasis, Rich barked orders to stay in line. "A very *straight* line."

Naz stole a glance into the window of a South Circle cabin, locking eyes with a reddish-brown-haired camper. *It's the girl from the cart!* Cocking his head, he slowed down. *She's crying.* Calliope music floated past as inexplicably as it had earlier in the day. He looked around, but nobody else seemed to hear it. By the time he turned back to the window, the girl's expression had transformed. She smiled and gave him a quick wave.

She remembers me too. Naz waved back. As she disappeared from view, he tripped, stumbling into the boy in front of him.

"Watch it." Ryan, who towered over Naz, shoved him backwards.

"*Je m'excuse,*" he mumbled, forgetting the English words.

Rich stood aside as the line moved past. "Follow directions," he said, raising his voice to add, "BOTH... OF... YOU."

After the counselor turned away, Ryan scowled at Naz. "Thanks for getting me in trouble."

Naz sped up to catch up with the others at a tall post covered with wooden arrows. One, marked BALL GAMES, pointed to an all-purpose field on the right.

"Who's up for softball first thing tomorrow?" Woody asked.

All ten boys raised their hands, even Naz, who had never heard of softball. He gazed longingly at some kids kicking around a fútbol but figured joining them for his favorite sport would probably break more of Rich's rules.

Another arrow marked PICNIC GROUNDS pointed left toward the cookout underway in an open grove with colorful tables. Rich marched everyone into the food line, and Naz filled his plate precariously full of a barbecued burger, corn on the cob, and beans baking in a large, bubbling vat. After devouring dinner, he pushed ahead of his cabin mates to be first in line for dessert.

"Vanilla ice cream? Chocolate? Coconut? Or some of each?" offered the server, but Naz pointed to the lime green treat labelled JELL-O, his eyes dancing as its surface quivered with each spoonful she dropped into his bowl. On the way back to the cabin's table, he encountered the sandy-haired, stocky boy from earlier. His plate was as full of Jell-O as Naz's.

Darby stuck to Sally and her other counselor, Rochelle, while the Six South girls waited in line for food. *I hope my eyes aren't red*, she thought, still puzzled about the weird music. Why had her tears instantly dried when the olive-skinned kid from the cart passed her window? After filling her plate, she hung back from the others and found a seat by herself at one of the picnic tables. Their turquoise, tangerine, and ruby hues reminded her of the grocery store ice pops her mother refused to buy.

She stared at her food, avoiding anyone nearby. Their animated conversations only sharpened the ache in her chest over losing Monica as a bunkmate. *Maybe my stutter bugs her after all.* As she pushed baked beans listlessly around her plate, she bit her knuckles to keep from crying again. Her mother's reprimand rang truer than ever. *The better you speak, the better off you'll be.*

"What are you doing over here, sweetie?" asked Counselor Sally, appearing from nowhere.

"Um. I-I-" Darby looked down, a lump growing in her

throat. "I guess I couldn't f-f-find anyone."

"You need to sit with the rest of us. Go on over there now. I'll be right back."

Darby sighed, hurrying toward her group. Fighting tears that clouded her vision, she tripped over a rock and crashed into two campers.

The collision sent their plates flying, scattering food everywhere.

Darby's stunned eyes latched onto theirs, one by one. *It's the kids from the cart.* "I'm sorry," she said to the sandy-haired, stocky one, "but I got baked beans on your leg."

The boys cracked up, and so did she, their laughter ringing out louder than the sounds from crowds of kids nearby. By the time they'd contained themselves and cleaned off, she added, "I'm Darby, by the way."

"My name is Naz," said the smaller boy, still shaking green Jell-O globs from his hair.

Darby turned to the older kid, who clamped his fist to his forehead, as if he were trying to remember something. She raised her eyebrows.

The kid's fingers opened, his arm dropping to his side. A funny expression spread over his face, like he was deciding. He cleared his throat. Finally, he spoke. "I'm Justin." It was almost a whisper. He cleared his throat again. "Justin Pennington," he said, his voice clear.

With that, blaring carousel music drove Darby's hands to her ears. She flinched. *No other kids are covering their ears, only these two guys.* "You heard that, right?" she asked.

"How could you not?" Justin chuckled, and Naz agreed. "Very loud."

"Whew," said Darby. "I thought I was going nuts. And I heard it before."

Justin nodded slowly. "So did I."

"I, too," said Naz.

Darby regarded Naz, struck by his blue eyes, then Justin, then Naz again. *Where is it coming from?*

Even though that thought remained in her mind, both boys replied at once, as if she had spoken. "I don't know."

"Did you just hear me think that?" The sudden goosebumps that raised the hair on the back of Darby's neck made her shiver. "What's going on?"

A whistle blew, and Naz sighed. "My counselor calls. I must return."

"Me too," said Justin.

Her mouth curved upward. "Me three."

They set off separately, but as Darby turned back to watch them go, two words ran through her head: *Operation L.U.C.K.* Her plans to include Monica, seemingly so important moments earlier, appeared to have changed.

When she returned to Six South's table, Lindsay slid over to make room for her. "Where have you been?" she demanded. "Not ool-cay."

"I-I-I..." Darby began.

Lindsay handed her a cookie with twinkling eyes.

Darby relaxed. "Not ere-hay," she giggled, and the two girls joined in.

"Thanks," said Darby when Monica offered her ice cream. *I guess she still likes me. And Lindsay's nice.* She stole a glance in their direction while they concentrated on a "rock, paper scissors" game. *If I go back to Operation L.U.C.K.'s orange building without Monica and put my feet in the cement circle horseshoes like we did last year, won't she be mad to miss what happens? She forgot our pledge to be bunkmates. Could she have forgotten Operation L.U.C.K. too?*

Monica yelled, "Rock. Ha, I win!" and Lindsay replied, "OK, we're tied. My turn."

Darby blew out her cheeks. *But if Monica remembered, wouldn't she have brought it up by now? She can't hear me think, like those boys do. Besides...* When she'd looked at Naz and Justin, the thought of Operation L.U.C.K. had lit up in her head like a neon sign.

Chapter Three

JUNE 15

The next day, as Darby and her cabin mates ambled down a winding path to a wooden dock by the lake, they tossed out ideas for a group nickname.

"What about Peppermint Patties?" said Darby's bunkmate, Austine.

"I still like Wild Strawberries," insisted Monica, and she raised her fist in triumph when it won the vote.

"No way," said June, provoking a snort from her twin, Jessica, who added, "Why not something even more ridiculous, like Watermelon Monsters?"

Counselor Rochelle, ignoring the sisters' grumbling, announced, "Welcome to the Lakeside Launch," and read the rules while the Wild Strawberries slipped into life jackets. "Number Ten," she concluded, "*always* stick with your 'team buddy' at the picnic grounds." She clapped her hands. "C'mon girls. Like I said last night, pair up with someone you don't know very well."

"Or not," whispered June.

Darby caught her winking at her sister. *Do they ever say anything that* isn't *sarcastic?* She relaxed her gritted teeth and reminded herself of the new plan she'd devised last night to implement Operation L.U.C.K. Alone. *For now.* Since the twins never left each other's sides, Darby banked on being able to sneak away more easily if she could get one of them to be her team buddy. She exhaled slowly. *Operation L.U.C.K., here goes.*

"J-J-Jessica," she said, hoping the twin she tapped on the shoulder wasn't June, "let's be buddies for this."

"I don't think so." Jessica smirked with her sister. "June and I are already buddies. Find someone else."

Counselor Sally intervened. "You heard Rochelle. It needs to be someone you don't know very well. Jessica, go ahead. Darby's your buddy."

Darby turned away to dodge what she suspected would be the twins' contemptuous expressions. *But the hard part's done.* She boarded a waiting canoe, stealing a glance at them. Sure enough, June and Jessica were already sitting beside each other. Darby squinted into the clear blue lake. Her smile broadened into a grin. The fractured reflection in the undulating water grinned right back. *Step one accomplished.*

"Hey," said June, pointing at a narrow band of sand that ran around the shore. "We could have just walked."

Did Rochelle just roll her eyes? Darby covered her smile. *Going by boat is way more fun.*

The rest of the Wild Strawberries leapt in one by one, and the shiny silver vessels swayed under their weight.

"Grab your paddles," Sally yelled. "Ready? Go!"

Less than ten minutes later, a big PARADISE PICNIC GROUNDS sign greeted them on the opposite shore. The counselors passed out lunch bags, reminding everyone to find their team buddies. Darby grabbed her sack then sat next to Jessica, across from June, at one of the forest-green wooden tables.

"What'd you get?" Jessica asked.

Darby opened her mouth to answer, but June replied, "Egg salad."

"I have turkey." Jessica handed half her sandwich to her sister, ignoring Darby.

Check! To keep from saying that out loud, Darby feigned fascination with her tuna sandwich, gobbling it down. Then, she slipped away.

Darby and Monica had dreamed up Operation L.U.C.K. during last year's Lakeside Launch. First, they'd discovered a white-lettered sign with an arrow pointing at a pathway. It read INLAND ROUTE BACK TO CAMP INCH. Locating the sign quickly, Darby wandered down the same pathway. *Forty-five minutes to go and come back.* She set her watch timer to count down, adding a fifteen-minute warning beep.

Her feet crunched on the pebble-filled path. Flowering bushes and maple trees surrounded her on both sides, their leaves rustling in the balmy breeze. The farther she went, the more overgrown the curving path became. *As if it hasn't been used in a long time. Maybe no one's been here since Monica and me.* She slowed to gulp some water from her canteen. *Should I be doing Operation L.U.C.K. alone?*

"Alone..." It echoed in her head. "You're alone far too much." The words stung, as if her mother shouted reprimands from the branches of every tree Darby passed.

Her throat tightened at the memory of their recent argument. She had sought refuge in her bedroom, slamming the door so hard that one of her riding trophies toppled off the shelf. When her dad came, Darby ran to him, burying her face in his shirt. "Why does she hate me?"

He'd gathered her in his arms, holding her on his lap in the rocking chair as if she were still a small child. "We both want the best for you, sweetie. Sometimes that ends up different from the way we mean it to sound," he said.

"I don't believe you," Darby had sobbed. "She n-n-never does anything wrong. She's p-p-perfect."

"Honey, your mom's not perfect. No one is."

"Well, she acts l-l-like she is." *She hates me when I stutter, for sure.* Leaving that unsaid, Darby had wiped away tears. *She's only nice when I win riding awards.* "I hate her!"

"Now, see," he said, his voice soothing the fury that had reddened her cheeks, "that's how it feels, but she loves you very much. And I know you love her."

Darby had tossed her arm around his neck and kissed him. *I wish Mom acted like Dad. He doesn't mind my stutter. And he always convinces me I can do things I think I can't.* Like the way he'd talked her into signing up for Camp Inch last year when all she wanted was to stay home.

Chattering blackbirds and blue jays pulled her back to her surroundings. The scent of wintergreen berries, bluebells, and wild sassafras from the bushes restored her resolve to continue by herself. She walked a bit faster up a steep incline, removing her official Camp Inch Sweatshirt and tying it around her thin waist.

At the hilltop, one sign pointing left read CAMP INCH VIA WHITE FALLS HIGHWAY: 1/4 MILE EAST. Another pointed right, cautioning PRIVATE PROPERTY! Her pulse quickened. She followed it past bushes and trees.

Below her, an orange football-field-sized building, dressed up with castle-like turrets at each corner, rose several stories high. Darby smiled with glee. *I found it!* Massive green letters spelling out "L.U.C.K." were painted on its side, glowing brighter than ever. A surrounding fieldstone wall led eastward toward camp.

She hurried down to a spot beside the immense wall where ten golden horseshoes sat lodged in concrete. *Same as when Monica and I found them!* The sun glinted on a colorless glass circle embedded above the horseshoes. Last time they'd rushed too much to notice the lines inscribed on it. Now, she knelt to read what they said.

All That We Give

Comes Back to Benefit Ourselves

With no time to figure that out, she placed her feet inside two of the horseshoes, like last year. Her heart pounding, she waited anxiously for the faint rumbling she and Monica had heard – or possibly imagined.

Will it even work without her?

The ground trembled ever so slightly beneath her.

She shivered with relief. *Yes, I feel it!*

Last year, their counselor came after them to end the adventure before it began. This time, the rumbling got louder. Darby ducked to avoid the small rocks and dust that fell from the stone wall looming above her head. Grating and creaking accompanied deep vibrations inside the fieldstone. A Darby-size section swung out on hinges, exposing a latch chain fastened to an old wooden door. She tried to remember to breathe. Or how to breathe. Overcoming the urge to back away, she yanked the chain, pushed the door open, and strained to see.

For a few seconds, semi-darkness that lay beyond kept her cemented in place. Finally, anticipation conquered her apprehension. *I can't stop now.* Electrified, Darby squared her shoulders and stepped inside.

The door slammed shut behind her with a bang. Lively carousel calliope strains, same as the whistling-type music she'd heard with Naz and Justin, accompanied a flash of gold, like shimmering fireworks.

She licked her dry lips. Her vision slowly adjusted to the dim rays streaming in from windows high above. A familiar aroma smelled so sugary strong she almost tasted it. *Like the smell that came from my suitcase on the weekend before camp.*

The light illuminated a solitary white carousel horse with a scarlet bridle. As if on a moving merry-go-round, it rose and dipped on its golden pole. Darby backed away.

What should I do? Get on? The calliope music got a little louder. Trembling but encouraged by the music, she moved forward and touched the horse. Relieved to feel solid wood rather than something alive, she slid her foot into its metal stirrup and hoisted herself up.

The horse rose again. Its pole disengaged from the stand and headed toward the high ceiling. Darby's mouth fell open. She threw her arms around its cool, smooth neck to keep her balance. *Am I floating? This can't be possible.* She shut her eyes, only to quickly open them again. *Yes, I am floating. Hold on!*

The horse traveled across the vast warehouse, moving slowly above stacks of wooden crates. She spotted an odd jumble of giant wooden blocks, more carousel horses, Ferris wheel seats, and piles of wooden Skee-Balls. *No one will believe me. This is better than anything Monica and I ever supposed would happen. If I tell her...* Darby took a deep breath, lightness bubbling up and down inside her. By this time, she had stopped shaking.

With a clank, the horse landed in another metal stand next to a cotton candy machine. *Cotton candy!* That's what's making the sweet smell.

"Hello?" Darby croaked. She waited.

A jangling sound, like a bunch of keys, answered.

"Hello?" she repeated, louder this time. "Is s-s-someone there?"

"Yes," a deep voice burst forth.

Darby froze.

"Welcome to Leroy Usher, Carnival King, young lady," boomed the voice.

Leroy for L, U for Usher, C for... like the green L.U.C.K. letters on the building. She took her time sliding off the horse. "Where are you? W-w-who are you?"

"I'm glad you're here," it said. "I compliment your intrepid, brave nature."

Darby's brows drew together as she tried to remember if anyone had ever used either of those words to describe her. *I doubt it.* Her mom had never said anything even close. She managed a reply. "T-t-thank you. That's nice."

"Indeed, it's true."

His unmistakable confidence made it seem like she'd known him for longer than just seconds. Something moved in the corner of her eye. She jumped, spinning around, only to find her reflection in a fun-house mirror being pulled apart like a life-size piece of taffy.

"I would be most grateful for your help." The kindness in his voice reminded her of the way her favorite teacher encouraged students last semester. "We can assist each other."

"Me?" she asked. Her watch alarm beeped. "Oh no, I have to g-g-go!" she cried.

"I invite you to come back another time," said the unseen presence. "Will you return?"

"Yes," Darby said, as eager to learn more as she was reluctant to depart. "I promise."

"Goodbye for now," the voice added. Only silence remained.

She climbed onto the horse. *Will it take me back?* To her

relief, it lifted off smoothly. She searched below to see if someone was really there, but nothing moved.

After the horse returned to its original stand, Darby slid down. Above, another flash of shimmering gold went off, and she found herself back where she started, her feet planted in the horseshoes outside. The wall stood blankly innocent, every stone in place.

When her heart stopped thumping and her legs no longer seemed stuck in quicksand, she bolted off and ran all the way back to Paradise Picnic Grounds.

Chapter Four

That same morning, Naz tore open a box from Mamá.

Dear Naz:

This package from Papá arrived, so I'm sending it to you overnight. Camp Inch seems like a wonderful place. I truly believe you will enjoy yourself there, my sweet boy.

Here, the unpacking continues. My recital last night went better than I could have hoped. What a joy it is to sing again!

I promise to write more in a few days.

Love from your Mamá

Naz breathed in the faint fragrance on her peach-colored stationery. Pulling out a gift box sealed with a Ministry of Tourism sticker, he ripped through layers of wrapping. *Doux Rêves – dozens of them!* He tossed a lime cordial in his mouth while unfolding Papá's letter, written in Arabic, unlike Mamá's, composed in French.

Son,

By now you will have arrived at your summer camp,

and I hope you are finding your accommodations pleasant. I thought you might enjoy your favorite candies, so I've sent a small supply.

Our home is very empty without you, but please do not be concerned about me. I remind you that your time in America means only that Mamá's singing career demands we must live apart for periods of time. And although I miss both of you deeply, we have asked you to remember that our love for each other remains unchanged and always will.

I must not forget to tell you that I saw your friends Qadir and Zed yesterday on my way to the embassy. They send their best regards.

Please write to tell me of all your activities.

Your devoted Papá

Naz gazed outside, carefully re-folding the letter and placing it alongside Mamá's under his pillow. He popped in another Doux Rêves, but its sweet taste failed to erase his sadness. *How long are "periods of time"? Mamá said it was "a joy" to sing. What if it means forever?*

At Woody's announcement to get ready for today's hike, Naz slid off his bunk, grabbing a handful of candies to share. He and his cabin mates filed outside into the humid morning to join boys from other groups on the tree-ringed plaza. As counselors passed out yellow caps, he waved to Justin.

With a whistle blast, Rich directed everyone past Branch Hall down a dirt road toward White Falls Highway. They crossed at a signal, traveled over some flatland and began climbing Mt. Sebastian.

Naz, his spirits restored at the prospect of a coming adventure, donned his new yellow hat with Camp Inch's name spelled out in log-shaped letters. Behind him, the line of boys with matching caps reminded him of a yellow serpent winding its way up the mountain. As they went, he and some cabin mates took turns pointing out patterns in the dirt path made by sunlight pouring through the twisted, leafy branches. Then they searched for landmarks in the terrain below. At the first switchback, Branch Hall still seemed relatively visible, but after a while, it had disappeared among the trees.

Before long, Rich's whistle screeched, bringing the hike to a halt. "It's 1200 hours," he bellowed, directing the campers onto a large, grassy clearing. "Thirty minutes for lunch."

"Eugene," said Justin to his bunkmate, "what's that white stuff on your arms?" Removing his yellow cap to wipe his forehead, he almost added, "It looks as goofy as your belt bag," but he changed his mind just in time.

"It's a special sunblock." Eugene pulled out a tube. "Works

great. Want some?"

After disguising his chortle as a cough, Justin tossed out a quick, "No thanks," then looked around for someone else to talk to.

Meeting Darby and Naz at the cookout had erased a self-imposed rule that demanded his silence over the last month. *I've said more in the last few days than I've spoken for months.* It felt nearly as good as the game-winning grand slam he'd hit when his dad coached Little League.

As campers waited in line for sandwiches then sorted themselves into smaller groups to eat, Naz came running over. Justin motioned him to a table by the mountain edge's fence.

"What is your sandwich?" asked the younger boy.

"Peanut butter and jelly."

"That sounds delicious." Naz sniffed doubtfully at his tuna fish.

Justin sighed. "You want to swap?"

With Naz's blissful smile as his reward, Justin gazed out over the endless terrain below, spying a splash of color. "What's that?" He pointed to a mega-size orange structure shining in the sunlight. It was surrounded by a wall that extended to the land where Camp Inch probably began.

"I do not know."

"It looks like it's next door to camp, but the wall is probably tall enough to block our view from the ground."

Without warning, the sky opened up with a heavy rainstorm. While the other campers scrambled for cover, Justin grasped the table, transfixed by the orange building. For a split second, it flashed with gold light, like shimmering fireworks. "Wow!" he burst out, "did you see that?"

Wide-eyed, Naz squeaked, "Yes."

Just as quickly as the rain started, it stopped. They stared at each other.

"You two okay?" Franklin, completely drenched, stopped in his tracks. "HEY, you're hardly wet!"

Justin felt his shirt. *Dry.* Naz's clothes were too. But he had a more fundamental question for the counselor. "What's that?"

Franklin followed Justin's finger to the orange building. "It's an old warehouse next to camp." A piercing blast from Rich's whistle distracted him. "Oh geez, Rich," he muttered, adding, "C'mon, we're heading back."

The boys gave each other another glance. *Did we really see it glow?*

As if he'd spoken out loud, Naz replied, "Yes."

"You heard me, right?"

Naz nodded.

Justin scratched his head, shooting Naz a quizzical look. Then they moved off, followed briefly but unmistakably by whistling carnival music.

Chapter Five

JUNE 16

Dear Justin:

I couldn't resist writing, even though you've been gone for only a few days. Do you remember Mrs. Nezri, the blonde woman from Morocco we met with her son, Naz? When I first saw her, I thought she was Scandinavian, but it turns out she was born in France. She's an opera singer. We both live in Milwaukee, and she invited me to her recital last night where she sang an aria from *Madama Butterfly*. It was nice having an evening out.

I finally finished decorating the O'Haras' place, after putting them off for so long. They couldn't have been nicer. I decided it's time to redo our house too. Your baseball card collection is safe, but I had to get rid of your popsicle sticks. They were attracting ants.

I miss you, dear. The house is not the same without you.

Much love,

Mother

From his wicker rocking chair on Branch Hall's porch, Justin held up the stick of the popsicle he'd just finished. His expression drooped, like he'd lost a best friend. *I could probably rebuild my collection.* He squeezed his eyes shut. *But what's she going to do with Dad's stuff?* As he broke the stick in half, Naz, crunching on a chocolate bar, emerged from the dining hall and sat next to him.

They rocked in silence, while bird tweets mixed with muffled conversation from a group of girls lounging on the side porch. Justin unfolded his letter, showing Naz the reference to his mom's opera recital.

The boy grinned between bites of chocolate. "*Madama Butterfly?* Is that about..." He reached for the words. "A large insect?"

"Probably not." Justin laughed, savoring the breeze and relaxing in his new friend's company. *Can he still hear my thoughts?* He turned toward Naz. *We never figured out why we didn't get wet in the rain.*

Naz, absorbed in licking his fingers, froze. "What?"

"I said..." Justin stopped. The soft sounds of a calliope seemed to hang in the air. Then he repeated it silently.

"Yes, it was a surprise that we did not become wet," replied Naz.

"That's crazy," said Justin. "You try it."

Naz wiped his fingers on his pants. *I would like to eat another candy bar.*

Justin snickered and pulled one out of his shirt pocket. He tested it again. *Orange.*

"Yes, orange."

Justin attempted to tug at his short hair, his voice rising in excitement. "Hey, did you hear any more about that big orange building we saw yesterday?"

He jumped when a female voice cried out, "WHAT?"

Darby, the girl they crashed into at the cookout, peered around the corner. "What did you say?"

Justin squinted at her. *What does she know about the orange building?* he thought to Naz, who shrugged.

Darby's mouth dropped open. "You *do* know about it, don't you? You said it again."

"I didn't say anything." Justin gulped.

"But I heard it anyway." Darby sank into a rocking chair next to him.

"And listen," Justin said, cocking his ear. "There's that magic music, like we heard the other night." He caught her eye. *Can you tell what I'm thinking?*

Darby turned pale. "Yes," she said.

A whistle screech jarred Naz to his feet. "Oh, no! I must go."

As he rushed off, Justin stared at Darby. Her mouth stayed closed, but he heard her voice.

Should I tell him about my adventure? Would he even believe me?

"Yes, I would," he insisted, his heart hammering.

"Wow, that is too… too… freaky."

His fingers tightened on his armrests. *Let's talk more at dinner.*

Okay.

Justin's mouth twisted into a smile, and he relaxed. *See you then.*

A little later, he kept watch out the window from atop his bunk with frequent glances at the bedlam around him.

Near the doorway, two cabin mates named Harper and Emmanuel attempted to race a pair of insects. From Justin's viewpoint, the bugs were not cooperating. A burly kid named Kenny showed off judo moves, striking the air in front of Eugene, almost half Kenny's size, who retreated to his bunk below Justin's. "I *hate* locusts."

"Huh?" Justin looked back at the insects. *Locusts?* "I'm pretty sure they're just grasshoppers." *Eugene's such a dork.*

Franklin and Ben entered the cabin, each brandishing fruit scoopers and other kitchen implements. "Well, there's a giant crate of watermelon with our name on it," Franklin announced.

"Plus more blueberries than you could ever imagine. Guys, somehow we're going to pull off making fruit salad."

"I'm checking my flashlight for a penknife," declared Hugh, while the other boys groaned, and Justin turned back to the window.

"Hey, Justin buddy," Ben called, "whatcha looking at?"

Justin shrugged. "Nothing."

"Well, how would you like to be lead chef for our contribution to the camp potluck tonight?"

"Me?" Calliope music turned Justin back to the window where Naz waved at him across the way. *At last!* He concentrated intently. *Meet Darby and me tonight at the camp potluck.*

I will be there.

Justin mimed a furtive thumbs-up then turned back to the counselors. "Sure." He slid down to join the rest of his group – now called the Charging Buffaloes – as they left for an adventure in Branch Hall's kitchens.

I'm sure of it, Naz thought as the calliope faded. *That music is magic! I hear it every time something amazing is about to happen. Like when I read Justin's mind. Or when he understands me even if I'm thinking French words. It played after the rainstorm when we saw that orange building. Maybe it's playing*

inside it. He looked around. *Who would know?* Probably not Rich, who gripped a potato, drilling several boys on the proper way to remove its peel.

Naz went to help Woody tack up a RICH'S RANGERS sign, the group's new name. Holding one of the edges while the counselor secured it with a tack, Naz spoke French to ask, "Have you ever seen the orange building next to our camp?"

"Sure, it's about a quarter mile down White Falls Highway." Woody scratched his chin and sat on his bunk. "The man who owned it, that was his warehouse. He built carnival rides and games."

Naz brightened. *Carnival rides? Probably with carousel calliope music!* He settled cross-legged on the floor in front of Woody. "Did you ever see inside?"

"Sure did. Back when I was a camper here, he invited Camp Inch kids to go on his rides. There was a Ferris wheel and a Tilt-A-Whirl and a big carousel. Mr. Usher made cotton candy for us, too."

"What is cotton candy?"

Woody chuckled gently and explained, while Naz's mouth watered at the idea of a treat made completely of sugar. "Mr. Usher was great. He had this big voice and he loved kids. He'd say, 'Welcome to Leroy Usher, Carnival King,'" Woody boomed, still speaking French.

"What happened to him?"

Rich cleared his throat, signaling Woody over for an animated conversation that ended when Woody stomped back. This time he answered Naz's question in English. "He died a few years ago."

"*Pour quoi est l'immeuble utilize...*" asked Naz, quickly switching languages too. "What is inside the building now?"

"I don't know," replied Woody.

We must find out. "When you visited, how did you arrive? Did you travel by car down White Falls Highway?"

"No, there's a gate in the wall between camp and Mr. Usher's property, and we walked over that way. I went back there one summer, but it was all locked up."

"Line up, men," instructed Rich, dumping his bowl of potato peels into a trash bag.

Naz rushed to get his yellow cap. *Does Darby know what Woody just told me? Someone must be playing the music!*

～∽～

That evening, as cooks ferried trays to long black barbecues, one of them muttering, "This place looks like a train station at rush hour," Darby helped deliver the Wild Strawberries' coleslaw to the potluck. Then she hurried to catch up with her cabin mates, who waited in line for dinner. After filling up on steak, corn, and an almost endless series of camper-made dishes,

Darby sat with Austine, almost hypnotized when the falling sun set the hills ablaze in reds and oranges.

Camp Inch's resident folk singers took the stage to kick off a sing-along, and Austine asked, "Don't you love 'Wind Beneath My Wings?' I hope they do that one."

Darby hesitated. Although her speech therapist had promised she wouldn't stutter while singing, she refused to try, so she didn't know many songs. Except one. "How about Johnny Rebeck, that creepy-funny one?" she replied, inducing shrieks of laughter from June and Jessica across the table. "Wh-wh-what's wrong with that?" Her cheeks hot, she rubbed her forearm, still sore from grating the coleslaw's cabbage and carrots.

"It's pretty ancient," scoffed June. "My grandmother taught it to me."

Counselor Rochelle shushed everyone for it to be quiet.

Midway through the program, after "John Jacob Jingle Heimer Smith," the singers struck up "Johnny Rebeck's" opening chords. Darby narrowed her eyes at the twins, anticipating the song's nonsensical lyrics. For a second, she imagined substituting "June and Jessica" for the cats and dogs who were ground to sausages in Mr. Rebeck's evil machine. *But ick.*

After the sing-along ended with, "That's What Friends Are

For," Darby escaped during cleanup, joining Justin and Naz at the ball field across the way.

"*En-fin*!" said Naz. In response to her, "Huh?" he translated, "At last. At last I can inform you..."

Before he could finish, Darby broke in with a question that had mystified her as much as the calliope music. "How did you know about the orange building?"

"We saw it on our hike up the mountain yesterday," said Justin. "There was a big gold flash, and we heard that funny music, too."

"The magic music..." Naz attempted, but Darby interrupted again.

"*I* saw a gold flash yesterday too, but I was *inside* the building." As she unfolded the tale and the genesis of Operation L.U.C.K., the boys listened, their mouths falling open.

Finally, Naz shared his news about Mr. Usher, frequently substituting French for English, and imitating a booming voice. "Welcome to Leroy Usher, Carnival King!"

"That's right, that's what he said! L.U.C.K. stands for Leroy Usher, Carnival King. Like the letters on the building. Get it?"

Naz, white as a sheet, gulped. "But Woody told us Leroy Usher is dead."

Her face clouded. "But if Mr. Usher is dead," she said quietly, "who talked to me yesterday?"

Neither boy offered an answer.

"I want to find out," she insisted. "I have to go back. I promised I would." Without saying a word, she made a decision. *Would you come with me?*

Both boys grinned. "Yes," said Naz.

"You heard me think that?"

They nodded.

"We'll go together," added Justin.

Darby's eyes lit up, but not for long. "How do we get there? We can't go from the picnic place across the lake, the way I did yesterday."

"We can try to find the gate in the wall between camp and the orange building, the one Naz's counselor talked about," suggested Justin. "Let's do it late tomorrow."

"At midnight," said Naz.

Darby's eyebrows rose. "Midnight?"

"Yeah, when no one's around," said Justin.

She took a deep breath. Disappearing during the picnic sounded much less risky than sneaking off at night. "I g-g-guess," she said. "Let me think about it."

Later, in bed, she went over the boys' idea. Her thoughts whizzed by like skateboarders speeding downhill, keeping her awake long past her cabin mates. *What if my mom finds out? What if anyone finds out?*

Mr. Usher's "intrepid" compliment rolled through her head, reminding her of the *Intrepid* aircraft carrier that Grandpa had shown her in a New York museum during spring vacation. He'd told her about serving on that very ship during World War II. She could still see his shoulders straighten with pride when he explained how he'd been scared to go into battle. "But guess what, honey?" he'd added. "I did it anyway."

THAT's how I want to be. Mom's not here. She can't stop me. And now, my two new friends want to go too. Quiet calliope music outside the window made her decision easy. As sleep overtook her, she curled onto her side. *It's settled. I'm going back to Mr. Usher's with Justin and Naz tomorrow. At midnight. Operation L.U.C.K., part two, launches with the three of us.*

On the next property over, the orange building appeared dark and quiet, but inside, the cotton candy machine began to glow.

Chapter Six

JUNE 17

Darby breathed in the smell of fresh hay as the Wild Strawberries arrived through a gate in the redwood fence that secured the equestrian area's several acres. She ran to the corral where Autumn Wind, his coat the color of a well-used penny, trotted over. "Hello, boy," she cooed, stroking the silky spot between the big bay mustang's nostrils. "Did you miss me?"

"He acts like he knows you," said Lindsay. "How do you tell one horse from the other?"

"It's easy," Darby answered. "See how the white on his nose looks like a dandelion?" She ran her hand lightly over the round marking above his big brown eyes, which narrowed to a stem-like line at his nostrils.

"Yeah. It kind of looks like a lollipop, too."

"You can usually tell them apart by those markings even if their coats are the same color."

"Darby knows everything you'd ever want to know about horses," said Monica. "Don't get her started, she'll never ut-shay up."

Darby laughed, wishing she could find fun friends like these at her strictly formal academy back home. Envisioning the pinched features, immaculate hair bun, and dark black riding jacket of owner Mrs. Thig, she wrinkled her nose. *Probably not.*

Counselors Sally and Rochelle helped sort everyone out, bringing novices to the tack room for basic lessons, while Darby, Austine, and bunkmates Sharon and Susan saddled up and took off on an "Advanced Equestrian" ride. Rochelle brought up the rear, appointing Darby to lead the way.

She chose a bridle trail where bushes with lilac and pink blossoms grew everywhere. As they approached the immense fieldstone wall marking camp's western property line, her eyes widened. *This is the wall that surrounds the L.U.C.K. building. We must be near the gate that Naz's counselor talked about.* "Don't tell anyone," she confided to Autumn Wind. "It's a secret. Operation L.U.C.K. continues at midnight."

Maybe I could *be intrepid like Mr. Usher said.* That morning, she'd looked up the word in Branch Hall's library to make sure it meant what she supposed. Although "fearless" came first on the definitions list, she noticed "determined" lower down. *I'm definitely not fearless. But maybe I am determined. At least here.* She tilted her head toward the sun. *If only camp lasted all year long, my mom couldn't tell me I'll never get anywhere if I stutter.* Her face reddened. *Does she think I do it on purpose?* Darby's grip tightened on the reins, doubt crawling up her arms. The breeze in her hair did nothing to blow away fear that her mom might be right. *I wish everything she says wouldn't bug me.*

Autumn Wind snorted and tossed his head. "Sorry, boy," she said, urging him on to a canter, leaving the others behind. "Didn't mean to ignore you."

When the trail turned shadier, Darby unhooked her helmet and wiped her forehead, damp from the blazing sun. On an adjacent path, at the end of a line of riders, Naz sat astride a pony, his features frozen in terror. A missing shoe on his left foot seemed to explain why two counselors were rummaging through the bushes. She rode up beside him. "Hi, Naz. Are you all right?"

Clutching his saddle horn, he didn't respond.

"See if you can loosen up a little and sit straight. Lean forward, like this."

"I can't," he cried, stiffening further. "I will fall to the ground. Like my shoe."

"Try it," she urged. "Trust me, you'll be okay."

He let go of the saddle horn and slackened his hold on the reins.

"Yeah, like that!" said Darby. "That's great."

"*Merci*," Naz grinned. "You are an instructive professor."

Darby chuckled. Before speeding off, she whispered, "Remember Operation L.U.C.K. tonight."

"Midnight," he affirmed. "I won't forget."

~~∞~~

MIDNIGHT...

Beep beep! Beep beep!

Darby startled awake and dove under the covers to silence her watch, poking her head out cautiously. The cabin remained still. With shoes and flashlight in hand, she slid down, crept outside on tiptoe, collected the backpack she'd hidden between a big rock and the cabin wall, and took off.

Using a long twig, she tapped on One North's window until Naz emerged. Justin, already awake when they reached him, swiftly joined them.

They stole past the cabins and ran to the cookout area, where they stuffed the pajamas they'd worn over their clothes into Darby's sack. Stashing it under a table, she dried her clammy palms on her shirt and took a deep breath. "Ready?"

Yes. The simple thought bounced from one to the other. Heaving shared sighs of relief, they went forward to search for a gate in the wall that separated them from L.U.C.K.

Darby led the way in silence along the dirt pathways, inhaling the intoxicating scent of jasmine. Warm air and the full moon's radiance encouraged her speedy steps. The closer they got to Camp Inch's western border, the fewer the trails. Branches and dried leaves crackled underfoot. Off in the distance, a nighthawk screeched. But when a pair of headlamps zoomed past, she held out a hand and slowed down. "This is wrong. We're going toward the highway, not west to the stone wall."

Faint calliope strains sounded in the night air. "Magic music," said Naz.

Darby pointed toward the sound. "Let's follow it." She resumed her rapid pace, rewarded almost immediately. Around a curve loomed the massive fieldstone barrier. "It's the wall," she exclaimed. "Now we just need to find the gate."

"Could be anywhere," said Justin. "The wall goes all the way around the orange building. We saw it on our hike. "

"Listen," Darby whispered. "Music again. C'mon!"

Seconds later, the calliope stopped, so they did too. She stuck the end of her flashlight through the ivy leaves that had overgrown the wall.

"That isn't stone," said Justin, "it's wood."

Darby brightened. "It's the gate!"

While Justin aimed his flashlight, she brushed away the foliage, exposing a thick iron handle midway up the planks that neither could reach. Naz gave the wood several forceful kicks. Nothing happened.

"Hello!" called Darby, her voice shaky. "It's me, I'm back!" Silence.

"We're pretty far from the orange building. What if he can't hear me?" Despite the warm evening, she rubbed her shivering arms. "What should we do?" Far off bells and rumbling from inside the wall silenced her. She froze, exchanging a wide-eyed stare with the others.

Justin bent toward the gate. "Whatever that is, it's coming this way."

Strong gusts sent leaves swirling in every direction.

"It's getting closer." Darby's uplifted gaze followed swinging beams of light that shot through ivy atop the wall, bathing it in an eerie brightness. She shielded her eyes and backed away, gripping the boys' hands.

Sparkling gold rocket-style fireworks exploded with a *bang.* Glittering X's in the sky flashed, popped, and sizzled. Then, with a burst of falling sparkles, a brilliantly illuminated trolley thundered over the wall. Its headlamps blinked. Bells pealed madly.

The gleaming green coach swooped down gracefully, landing next to the kids among puffs of pebbles and dust. They remained rooted in place. The trolley was quite unoccupied.

Darby circled it; her expression watchful. She looked from Justin to Naz. *What should we do?*

Naz shook his head, but Justin mimed stepping onto the gold-trimmed vehicle.

A creaking wooden stepstool unfolded to the ground. "All aboard," boomed a voice.

"It's *h-h-him*," Darby squeaked.

"All aboard!" the voice repeated.

She took one look at the boys' flushed faces, her heart pounding. "Now or never, right?"

They ran up the steps, settling onto plush gold velvet cushions atop rows of polished wooden seats.

Clang! Clang! went the front bell. *Clang! Clang!* echoed the bell in back. With that, the trolley's whooshing engines propelled its passengers, quaking with excitement, up into the night air and ferried them rapidly over the wall.

When they landed beside the mammoth orange structure, Darby, still stuck to her seat, grasped one of the trolley's handrails. "Mr. Usher? Are you there?"

As if in response, carnival music drifted from a pair of barn-like wooden doors, and the stool creaked to the ground.

"Should we go in?" asked Justin.

Darby squinted at the doors. "There's an envelope on the cross bars." She stepped down, followed by Justin. Naz waited behind.

When she picked up the envelope, a black-and-white

photograph of a young girl stared back from its face. "This is me. Where'd it come from?" She pressed her ear against the wooden doors.

Justin held the envelope up to the trolley's lights. "Your hair looks like a wig."

"Yeah, that's weird." Darby bent closer. "My hair is curly, not straight like that." She ripped it open. The parchment-like paper inside contained uneven, red text that appeared to have been made by an aged typewriter, the kind her class once saw at a printing museum. "'Welcome back,'" she read, her voice trembling. "'Please come inside and enjoy my carnival. I will join you soon.'" She raised her eyes from the letter. "It's from Leroy Usher."

Naz squeezed his eyes shut. He clenched his fists. "How can that be? He is dead."

While Justin got the doors open, she grabbed Naz's arm and pulled him behind her. "Come on."

Before crossing the threshold into a narrow room, lit by a plain fixture, Darby swallowed hard, Naz's question echoing in her head. Bare cement floors and factory-gray walls offered nothing except a closed-door reading OFFICE OF LEROY USHER in white lettering. She peered around.

Darkness showed through an archway encircled by lamps. But then carnival music floated through the air. The brilliant lights sprang on with a loud crack, bringing a gigantic space beyond to life.

Darby blinked at the brightness. She and Justin edged through the arch to a wide brick walkway lined with game booths and galleries, while Naz lagged a few steps behind.

So vastly changed was the space from the dim clutter she'd seen on her last visit, it made Darby almost forget she'd been there before. She craned her neck at the massive floor-to-ceiling murals decorating the walls. Their sunny skies and billowing clouds painted the illusion of an outdoor afternoon in perfect weather.

Motioning the others down a gravel walkway that crossed their path, Darby lobbed them an astonished glance. "Look at all this." She pointed at the whimsical storefront facades dotting its rims.

With a whoop, Naz pushed past. He turned his head every which way, carefully pronouncing the names on their animated signs. "Flying Dutchman Skyway. Undersea Octopus Dive. Sunset Safari, River Caverns, Bumper Boats, Storybook Castle."

"It's like the old-fashioned carnival they build every summer in our city park," said Justin. "You know, before stuff like lasers and video games were invented."

The circling Ferris wheel and spinning Tilt-A-Whirl made Darby dizzy. She shifted her gaze to an elaborate sign spelling out TIMELESS VOYAGES in flashing neon letters of crimson, amber, and cobalt blue. Then she lit up at an array of stuffed animals behind the PRIZES banner atop a row of Skee-Balls games. *Like Dad showed me how to play at our school bazaar.* "This way."

She landed only two of the dozen that she tossed into the Skee Ball rings then joined the boys next door at Milk Bottle Madness. Every metal sphere Justin threw at a line of containers hit its mark. When he finished, a mechanical machine issued sixteen little red prize tickets stamped L.U.C.K.

Naz wandered across the walkway toward a red cart and sniffed at its puffy cloud-like contents. "Cotton candy!" The sign read FRESHLY SPUN: 5 PASSES EACH. After he eagerly eyed his buddy's red L.U.C.K. tickets, Justin fed fifteen into the slot, pocketed the last one and handed around the pink cones.

Darby, her face as expectant as Naz's, hesitated, recalling her mother's caution about how sweets ruin your teeth. But since nothing at L.U.C.K. seemed quite real, she dug in and savored every bite that melted on her tongue. They ate in silence while the carnival whirled, whistled, and swirled around them.

"I know this aroma." Naz sniffed again. "It reminds me of something peculiar in my bedroom on the Saturday before camp."

"I smelled something sweet that day," Darby said slowly.

"Me too," echoed Justin.

How can that be? The thought passed between them.

"No clue." Darby shook her head. She tossed her cone into a clown-shaped trash bin's mouth.

"Thank you!" it responded.

Naz bent his face into the opening. "Mr. Usher?"

"Doesn't sound like him," Darby laughed. "Let's keep going." She set off past the games. Around a corner lay a spectacular merry-go-round, its calliope blaring even before they made the turn.

"There!" said Naz, jumping up and down.

The closer they got, the brighter the carousel glowed. Elegant mirrors reflected Darby's knowing smile as the calliope's trilling organ, bass drum, and crashing cymbals played their "magic music." She stepped aboard for a better view of the painted flowers on scenic landscapes, so realistic that she imagined them growing.

Four rows of horses circled the wooden platform. Some held galloping poses while others pranced or stood proudly still. Naz clambered onto one with peach and blue ribbons threaded through its mane. Justin picked a shiny stallion nearby. Darby, sidestepping the scarlet-bridled white horse she'd ridden across the warehouse last time, ran to a copper-colored Morgan resembling Autumn Wind.

Lost in thought as she strapped herself onto its saddle, like the Western ones worn by horses at camp, Darby could just hear her mother complaining to Camp Director Donna Inch. "You should really provide classically English-trained horses for advanced riders like my daughter." *That's what matters to Mom. The perfect English saddle. If she were here right now, it's probably the only thing she'd notice.*

The horse moved beneath her. "Wait." She gulped. "Did the carousel just start?"

Justin laughed along with Naz. "It's been going for almost a minute."

Darby wrinkled her nose. "I admit it, I was thinking about something else." Fully attentive, she grasped the golden pole.

Every revolution revealed one ride after another, and Naz read off their names. "Wild Whirlpools. Ring of Fire, Ali Baba's Forty Thieves." Sounding very much at home, he turned to the others. "My Papá loves reading *Ali Baba's Forty Thieves* to me."

"There's one called Hamlet's Haunted Forest. Hamlet, like Shakespeare?" Darby's giggle died as the merry-go-round sped up.

The outer row of horses pulled away from the platform. It swung free, clanking into an angled orbit with a thump matching the one in her chest. Increasing velocity drowned out the music.

"What's happening?" yelled Justin, hanging on to the pole.

"I don't know!" she called, even more alarmed by sudden pressure on her skull, like someone had fastened a giant rubber band around her forehead and tightened it. Her vision blurred into a riotous haze. As the turning got faster and faster, she grabbed her middle. *I better not throw up.*

Naz clutched his horse's neck. "Will we explode?"

With a grinding shift of gears, the carousel lifted off from its base. The spinning slowed, and the whirring quieted down. The outside row of horses fell back to its original position.

"We're flying… again!" cried Darby.

Justin gasped. "We're shrinking!"

Darby's horse whizzed past Wild Whirlpools, now a hundred times the size it had been seconds ago. The miniaturized carousel navigated across the warehouse, soared out its doors, passed over the fieldstone wall, and climbed up to the star-spangled sky.

From nowhere, a handsome, older man appeared on the carousel platform. His booming voice rang out. "Welcome to Leroy Usher, Carnival King."

Too stunned to say anything, Darby stared into his kind blue eyes. Her heart leapt into her throat. *Mr. Usher!* If she had tried to imagine exactly what Leroy Usher looked like, this would be it.

He wore a cropped red bolero jacket sporting big gold buttons, ivory pants tucked into sparkling black boots, and white gloves. The big top hat perched on his wavy black hair added to his height. He bowed, as if to reassure her. "I'm glad you came back."

"Th-th-thank you." She smiled shyly, unable to think of anything more to say.

"He's real," whispered Naz.

"I know!" Darby whispered back.

Mr. Usher shook hands with the boys, then he stood placidly and stared out.

What's he looking at? Darby tore her gaze from him, but she couldn't see anything other than the boundless midnight-blue sky. The wind rushed past her ears. *Like when you stick your head out a moving car window.* She leaned forward. Only a sprinkling of lights below gave her a sense of their distance from the ground.

"This is like the view from my airplane window when Mamá and I arrived in America," said Naz.

"Where are we going?" Darby asked.

"Langton Township," said Mr. Usher.

Darby shared a blank look with Justin.

The descent began. Lights turned denser. They flew past a village square with a courthouse, steepled churches, and groups of shops and single-story structures. By comparison, Darby felt tiny, perhaps the size of an orange. *Too small for anyone on the ground to see us. I hope.*

After circling a residential development of cul-de-sac neighborhoods, they touched down with a hiss and a jolt. Darby realized her mouth was wide open. In short order, she closed it. *We've landed on the roof of a house.* Her eyes got wider. *On top of a house.* "Wh-wh-what's keeping us from slipping off?"

Mr. Usher seemed unconcerned. He sprang open a large gold pocket watch, twisting the dial backwards. It ticked inconsistently, like a broken metronome.

"Look!" shouted Darby. The dark sky melted from midnight blue to violet, then red, orange, and yellow.

Soon, a sunny morning greeted them. Mr. Usher placed the watch back in his pocket.

"Sorry," she said. "I'll be quieter, so no one knows we're here."

"That's fine." Mr. Usher laughed heartily. "No one can hear or see us."

"Why not?" When she received no reply, she stole a glance at Justin. *How did he do that?*

He shook his head. *How does he do any of this?*

Darby swung her leg into a side-saddle position for a better view of the house below. It seemed still. But soon a tall, slim woman in an enormous sunhat appeared below them, busy pruning the overflowing pink roses, a wicker basket over her arm. Her forest green pants, held up by suspenders, drew Darby's admiration. So did the long brown braid intertwined with a white ribbon that hung down the back of a white T-shirt.

"Who's that?" she asked.

Mr. Usher beamed. "Her name is Katie."

Darby looked at Justin and Naz, her brows knitted. Both boys shrugged.

The front door of the house next to Katie's opened. Out walked a man with spiky, sandy hair, dressed in a tan business suit and dark sunglasses, absorbed in a mobile call. Flipping the phone shut, he set his briefcase on the passenger seat of the black car in his driveway.

"Nice Porsche," gawked Justin.

"That's Geoff," said Mr. Usher, "off to a hectic day in his law office."

Katie removed her hat, but instead of greeting her neighbor, she turned abruptly and disappeared inside her house. Catching sight of her expression, Darby murmured, "She looks so angry."

Mr. Usher said nothing, but when Katie's front door slammed, he stepped backward as if feeling its force.

A whistled tune turned their attention to the house beside Geoff's, where a dark-skinned man in blue denim work clothes, toting a lunch box, locked the front door.

"And that's Chad," said Mr. Usher, his tone subdued.

Geoff gunned his engine loudly, backed out of the driveway, and zoomed off.

Chad, the dark-skinned man, stopped whistling, staring after the car. After a moment, he drove away in his pickup truck.

"They don't seem to like each other very much," said Darby, who bit her tongue when Mr. Usher momentarily closed his eyes. *Maybe I shouldn't have said that.*

"Perhaps they do not know each other," suggested Naz.

"They do know each other, Naz," said Mr. Usher. "But you're right, Darby, they don't like each other. In fact, it's worse than I thought."

"Who are they?" said Justin.

Mr. Usher waited a moment before answering. "People I knew long ago." The sadness in his voice contrasted markedly with his normally spirited tones.

Darby frowned, struggling for something to say. Then she remembered his request from her first warehouse visit. "You asked for my help. What can I do?" The boys nodded as she added, "We all want to help."

"Thank you," he replied, bowing slightly. "I will explain thoroughly when we get back."

Producing the watch, he turned the hand forward. The sky's

sunny yellow dissolved to orange and red, then violet, and then dark blue, until it became night once more. With another hiss and a jolt, the carousel rose, and Mr. Usher's watch snapped shut.

They flew back into the warehouse, where the same odd rubber-band pressure on Darby's skull that accompanied their departure resumed, as did the frenetic circling. After it halted, and her head stopped spinning, she opened her eyes. The carnival looked like it had before.

Darby slid down from her horse and grabbed onto its pole for balance, hoping she could walk without falling over.

As Mr. Usher took them back to the foyer, Naz placed his palm atop his head then moved it across to Justin's shoulder. "Am I as tall as I was before we left?"

"You certainly are," said Mr. Usher. "Maybe a little bit taller," he added with a wink and invited them into his office. Its paneled walls, gleaming with light from green fixtures, contrasted with the stark gray hallway.

While Darby perched on one of three cushioned chairs in front of an L-shaped desk, Justin and Naz knelt on the carpet, their fingers tracing colorful wild animals in the pattern. "C'mon," she hissed at them, gesturing at them to join her.

"Take your time, young men," said Mr. Usher. He settled himself in a swivel chair behind the desk with a smile at Darby.

"My children enjoyed the carpet exactly as they do."

Darby blinked at the red telephone beside him. *Why does it have a round thing with holes where push buttons should be?* She tilted her head toward an ancient-looking typewriter on the desk. When the boys got up and plopped onto their chairs, she whispered to Justin, "Do you think he used that to type my message?"

"Maybe."

Her eyes roved around the room, freezing at a wall portrait behind Mr. Usher. It pictured a woman whose yellow dress set off her dark skin. She posed with her arms draped around three children.

"Mr. Usher," said Darby, gaping at the little girl in a pastel party outfit. "That's me! Like the photo on the envelope you left for me."

"It's all of us," said Justin. "Isn't it? Except for the hair."

"That is a painting of my wife and children. But," Mr. Usher added, his mouth curling into an affectionate smile, "I do see the resemblance."

"Where is your wife?" Naz asked. "May we meet her too?"

"She is not here."

"You must miss her. Even more than I miss my Papá," said Naz with a catch in his voice.

"She is in a different world entirely."

"Another country?"

"No," said Mr. Usher, clearing his throat, "although she was born in India."

"I think he means she passed away," whispered Darby, and Mr. Usher nodded. Out of the corner of her eye, she noticed Justin staring at the floor, as if he couldn't imagine something so sad.

Mr. Usher swiveled around. "We had this painted well over twenty years ago."

Twenty years ago? They're grownups now. Darby let out a gasp of recognition. "Those people we just saw -- they're your kids," she said to Mr. Usher. The anger on the woman's face and the way they ignored each other brought her to tears.

"Yes," he replied, his voice quiet. "Geoff, Katie, and Chad."

"Why are they mad at each other?" Darby chewed on her lip. *I probably shouldn't have asked.*

He fiddled with a round glass paperweight. "The strife between them brings me to the present. I can't rest," he added, so quietly it sounded like he was talking to himself, "until this property is again filled with happy children." He turned to the portrait. "Like my sons and daughter were back then." Swiveling back around, he handed the paperweight to Darby. "Do you see what this says?"

An orange streak, the same color as the building, circled one-quarter of its edge. She studied the words encased in the smooth round glass. "'All That We Give," she said, reading the black lettering out loud, "'Comes Back to Benefit Ourselves.'" *Where have I seen this before?* She flashed back to the horseshoes she'd seen outside the warehouse on her Lakeside Launch visit. *That's what it said on the glass circle above them. Is this the same one?*

Darby turned the paperweight over. *There was no orange streak then. I would have noticed.* "What does it mean?" she asked. "Like when we donate our stuff to the clothing drive?"

Mr. Usher seemed to be hiding a smile. "Somewhat. As a condition of returning to this world and obtaining your help, I must in turn help the three of you."

"Help us with what?" asked Darby.

"Perhaps we don't believe in ourselves," Mr. Usher inclined his head at her. "There are so many things we think we can't do. But we are, in fact, capable of more than we suspect."

Darby blushed. *How can he know that's what I think?*

"Perhaps we miss someone, like your Papá," he said to Naz, "and it makes us terribly unhappy until we can see them again." To Justin, he added, "Or maybe it's someone who can't come back, and we don't know how to make it right again."

Justin shifted in his chair, clenching and unclenching his fists. Darby caught his eye, mouthing, "What?" but he looked away.

Mr. Usher took back the paperweight. "If I am to return to

my wife, we must expand this orange crescent until it becomes a full circle. The color grows around the edge as we help each other."

"How?" asked Darby, her brow furrowed.

"You've already begun helping me by coming here. And I've begun helping you. When you heard my carousel music, something happened, didn't it?"

"Yeah, that's how we met," she said to the boys. "And we heard each other's thoughts."

"Correct. That's when this orange color appeared, but you could barely see it. When you helped me by coming here the first time, young lady, the orange line grew more." He pointed his index finger in their direction. "It also works when you help yourself by doing something you don't want to do. Or something you don't think you can. For some reason, that's when the color grows the most."

Darby shot a glance at Justin, who shrugged. "I'm not sure I understand," she said.

"For now, all I ask you to remember is that everything you experience here is of little value unless you bring it back with you into your lives. Eventually, I hope to give each of you something you want very much."

"What happens if we can't complete the circle?" she asked.

"Well, let's say that I will remain here until we do." Mr.

Usher looked toward his wife in the portrait, adding softly, "Or forever, if time runs out."

Darby's stomach fluttered, as if live butterflies had somehow gotten inside. *Forever? That sounds bad.*

He turned back to the kids. "So, will you return another time?"

"Definitely," she said, and the boys agreed.

"Good, good." Mr. Usher's voice had returned to full volume. He escorted them to the trolley. "I will be in touch soon."

Darby boarded last, stopping short. "The paperweight!" she exclaimed, pointing to where it sat on one of the gold velvet cushions. "How did it get here?" She turned to ask Mr. Usher if he wanted it back, but he had disappeared inside.

Justin picked up the paperweight then handed it to Naz. "Should we go ask him?"

Before Darby could reply, the bells clanged, the engines rumbled, and the kids held on tight. The trolley took off, sailed back over the big wall, and returned them to Camp Inch's solid brown earth just before dawn.

Chapter Seven

JUNE 18

Naz woke up and looked around, finding his blanket halfway off the bed as usual and the same early risers talking in the cabin doorway. Outside, a flock of squawking birds crossed the sky. *Did I dream last night? What about the paperweight? Is it still there?* His hand flew under the pillow, nearly knocking it off the end of the bed. As he clamped both palms around the glass and searched for a better hiding place, he shivered. *It was not a dream. It really happened.*

Justin replayed last night in his head, a million miles away from the dining room food line.

"C'mon, Pennington," said Harper, giving him a nudge. "Keep moving."

Justin blinked at his cabin mate as if they'd never met then grabbed a plate of Eggs Benedict. He reached into his pocket and turned over a breakfast voucher to the clerk.

"What the heck is this?" she asked, examining the red L.U.C.K. prize ticket.

The color fled from Justin's face as he snatched it back, replaced it with a camp voucher, and hurried off.

Darby had tossed and turned after creeping back into bed. Sitting drowsily on her bunk, holding one shoe in her hand and staring at the other on the bed, she couldn't stop thinking about Mr. Usher's words about time running out. Or his kids. *Why are they mad at each other?*

"You're so quiet this morning, Darby," called Monica. "I mean, not that you're ever a blabbermouth or anything. What's up?"

She looked up, tempted to confide about last night's adventure. *Or not. Monica never mentioned Operation L.U.C.K. Maybe she didn't think it was a big deal.* Darby hoped so, anyway. At last, she said, "I g-g-guess I had some pretty wild dreams."

"Well, c'mon, Lindsay's waiting outside."

Darby finished tying her shoes and ran to join them. *I'm really glad we're not bunkmates after all. It turned out perfect the way it is. Justin and Naz smelled the same cotton candy I did. We look like his kids, we all heard the same music, and we can read each other's thoughts. I know Mr. Usher means Operation L.U.C.K. for the three of us.*

The minute the Wild Strawberries arrived at Branch Hall, encountering a long line for breakfast, Darby scanned the room for Justin and Naz.

"We should have come earlier," griped June.

"Never mind, there's plenty of food," said Rochelle, digging in her backpack. "Oh shoot. I left the vouchers in our cabin."

"Want me to go back for them?" asked Sally.

"No, that's okay, Donna will give us more."

"May I get them from her?" asked Darby, seeking a few minutes to find the boys. "I-I-I have to pick up a magazine from the stack by her office."

"Sure, thanks," said Rochelle. "We'll wait for you in line."

Darby ran off, slightly conscience-stricken over her remark about magazines. She'd seen them somewhere in Branch Hall, but she'd never been anywhere near Donna's office. When she turned into the hallway that led there, she heard the director's voice describing a camp fair later in the summer and crept forward.

"Every cabin will have a booth for food, or fortune-telling, or games, that kind of thing. Too bad Leroy Usher's not around anymore. I bet he would've loaned us some of his carnival games."

"Mr. Usher?" Darby's mouth dropped open. She covered it quickly when a man appeared in the office door.

"Hello there," he said. "I'm McKendrick, Donna's new assistant director. What can we do for you?"

After Darby got her replacement tickets, she left the office but snuck back to eavesdrop in the hallway.

"Who's Leroy Usher?" McKendrick was asking.

"Leroy Usher! Well, he was a wonderful man," replied Donna, while Darby imagined the director peering at her colleague over her eyeglasses. "He designed and built amusement park rides in his warehouse on the next property over."

"That big orange place?"

"Yep," said Donna, "A year or so before he died, Leroy told me he would like his property to become part of this camp one day. So when he passed, I met with his daughter and sons to talk about buying it from the estate. They live right next door to each other in that Langton Township development with all the cul-de-sacs."

That's where we went last night! This time, Darby managed to keep silent.

"So what happened?" asked McKendrick.

"Nothing at this point. When I didn't hear back, I tried to contact them. The only one I could reach was the younger son, who told me they'd had an argument about what to do with the property. He wouldn't give me any details, but it sounded like his brother, who's an attorney, is the executor and wants to sell to a developer with plans to tear down the warehouse and build condos."

Oh no! Darby wondered how long she could hold her breath.

"They're lovely people, like their father," Donna added. "They need to talk through their differences so we can work out a deal to make that property part of the camp. Just like Leroy Usher wanted."

Mr. Usher's lawyer son. *What was his name?* Darby pushed her fist against her temple, as if that could help her remember. *The one with the briefcase and fancy car.*

"If anyone can close that deal, I'm sure you can."

"Why, thank you, dear," she said. "I'm going to contact them again."

McKendrick's chair moved, and Darby scurried away, pausing in the kitchen doorway to gather her thoughts.

I have to make sure Mr. Usher knows about this. If his son tears down the warehouse before we complete the orange circle, he's stuck here, and he'll never see his wife again!

Chapter Eight

JUNE 19

Chad Usher climbed into his pickup truck and tossed his cap onto the passenger seat. Perspiration wrinkled his shirt, so crisply fresh minutes ago. Twisting on the air conditioning, he backed out of the driveway into the deserted street. Not even Katie, who gardened every summer morning, was there in today's relentless sun.

Since their quarrel earlier this year in Pop's office, Geoff, Katie and Chad had avoided each other. *It's weird how we were all outside at the same time on Thursday.* The fresh sorrow that erupted when his brother ignored him still stung. So when Donna Inch phoned yesterday, he'd accepted her invitation to visit, figuring something might come of it.

Without much traffic, he arrived on White Falls Highway at the billboard reading CAMP INCH ENTRANCE and checked his watch. *Forty minutes early.* L.U.C.K.'s road lay just beyond. After the argument with his siblings, he'd avoided going there. *But maybe it's been long enough.* On a whim, he drove on and turned onto Carnival King Way.

Chad's stiff shoulders loosened when he approached the wall surrounding the warehouse. As full of anticipation as the child he was when Pop first brought him here, he got out and gazed up at the orange building's vibrant green letters and the turrets rising above the fieldstone. He kneeled at the golden horseshoes in the concrete beside the wall, running his hand over the U-shaped pieces. Even in the fieldstone's shadows, they seemed to gleam brighter than when Pop had laid them in honor of Mother after her death.

Hey. Where's the glass with Pop's favorite poem? He gaped at the empty circle in the concrete. "All That We Give to Others," he recited from memory, "Comes Back to Benefit Ourselves." *Who would steal that? And how would they get it out?* He glanced around, but nothing else looked as if it had been disturbed.

Pulling out a tangle of keys, Chad found one for the wrought-iron gate, drove in, and parked beside the barn-like doors. When he swung them open, warm air rushed out, hitting him in the face. He inhaled deeply. *After all these years, this place still smells like cotton candy.*

Sun poured through high windows inside the foyer, lighting his path. While he searched for the key to Pop's office, strains of muffled music and children's voices filtered out from deep in the warehouse.

He froze. *Is that a radio?* His heart racing, he moved toward the sounds, nearly tripping on an arch of lights on the floor beside an open door. Sign parts inside blocked his every step. "Octopus," read one. "Voyages," "Caverns," "Dutchman," read others. Pallets stacked with bricks, Ferris wheel seats, and boxes of Skee-Balls rested in no particular order as he passed. Eventually he stopped, his path obstructed by a couple of sky-blue tarp rolls.

Chad caught something moving out of the corner of his eye. He spun around. "Who's there?"

Staring back was his wavy reflection in a fun-house mirror propped against a crate.

Relaxing, he raised his arm. The reflection did too. Lifting his other arm produced the same result. Then he stood still, not daring to breathe, yet something moved in the mirror. The music and voices got louder.

At first, Chad squinted. Then his eyes grew wide. A girl with reddish-brown curls on a copper-colored Morgan was giggling about Hamlet and Shakespeare, her words too garbled to be understood. A smaller olive-skinned boy, atop a white Arabian with a peach and blue bridle, pointed off in the distance. "Ali Baba's Forty Thieves," he said. Nearby, a sandy-haired boy on a carousel stallion rose up and down, slightly distorted by the curved Plexiglas.

Katie never wore her hair curly like that. But those kids sure resemble the three of us. Their reverberating voices encircled him. *Where is that coming from?* He looked around, wiping his damp palms on his jeans. Nothing showed up behind him except dusty crates. *What's going on?* Soon, the warehouse went silent.

Chad sank down on a box. *Carnival King was our second home. When we were here, we felt just like that, so happy and carefree.*

Back then, Pop had brought them to the warehouse to play arcade games while he caught up on paperwork. Occasionally, he unveiled a surprise. Like the cotton candy machine. Or the contraption he rigged with merry-go-round horses, exactly like the ones in the mirror. In later years, the "contraption's" patent produced such a windfall that he'd bought them houses next door to each other in a cul-de-sac. "See?" he'd boom of his latest feats. "All things are possible."

"What about resolving this place's future?" said Chad, wishing Pop could hear. "That's what we fought about."

Donna's offer had sounded fine to him. His sister, however, balked at the modest price, and his brother wanted to explore a lucrative deal proposed by a developer. With no one willing to compromise, they'd begun arguing. He shuddered at the memory. Katie called him reckless with their money. He threw some profanity her way. Then Geoff escalated it further, threatening a lawsuit unless they agreed to his plan. After that, they'd stopped speaking.

But Pop always had a solution. Chad ticked off ways his father embodied the glass circle's poem about helping others. *I wouldn't have tried contracting without all he taught me. Geoff was ready to give up after failing the bar exam, but Pop stayed up many nights helping him study. When Katie wanted to become a teacher, Pop showed her how to get over being afraid to speak in front of people.* He choked up at the memory of Pop's words that came with every good night kiss: "Be good to one another."

The laughing kids materialized again in the mirror. "What would Pop tell us now?" he asked them.

The sound faded, and they disappeared.

Chad realized he already knew the answer. Leroy Usher's wishes couldn't be more obvious.

After locking up, he quickly drove to Camp Inch, where Donna waited on Branch Hall's steps. "Mr. Usher," she said. "Good to see you again. Thanks for coming."

"Call me Chad." They went into her office, closing the door behind them.

One quarter mile away, inside Leroy Usher, Carnival King, children's laughter and music resumed, louder and happier than ever.

Chapter Nine

JUNE 22

Dearest Naz:

It's not even a week since you've been at camp, but it seems longer. I have spent a great deal of time imagining what you're doing.

My concert with the symphony is next week. I'm so happy to be performing again, and I anticipate the day you can be in the audience to hear me sing.

I miss you a great deal, but I am confident that your experience this summer is a wonderful chance for you to practice your English and meet some new friends. I think it's easier, Naz darling, to learn new customs, not to mention a different language, when you're around other children. I studied English while growing up, but when I met Papá and moved to Morocco to marry him, I found it much more difficult to learn Arabic as an adult.

Being apart from home, Papá, and me cannot be all that easy for you. I understand how it feels to be thrust into a new culture. But like me, you are an adventurous soul, so I am filled with hope that you are thriving on all the wonderful new experiences you must be having.

Please write to me and to Papá when you have time.

Love,

Mamá

P.S. I've discovered a sweet little bistro nearby. They have your favorite kind of salmon rillettes, a marvelous chicken Basquaise, and scrumptious desserts.

Naz pocketed the letter, contentedly polishing off a hot dog at lunch. *I hope she will learn how to cook Jell-O and all the other wonderful camp specialties.*

～∾～

That morning, as the Wild Strawberries rode a Camp Inch school bus to Barton Flats for a day trip, Darby and Monica made plans to head for Allison's Attic before the dollhouse museum got too crowded with tourists.

"Don't you want to go to the Candy Basket?" asked Lindsay. "I heard the whole place smells like chocolate."

"Besides," June chimed in, "dolls are for babies."

"No," exclaimed Darby, "these are d-d-doll *houses*."

"Right, houses for d-d-dolls," she countered, then giggled

with Jessica.

"Never mind," said Monica, catching Darby's narrowed eyes. "We're going there first."

Soon, the bus pulled in at the village's old-fashioned Main Street, light years away from the camp's rustic surroundings. With instructions from counselors to meet in an hour at Cherry Gables Tea Room, the three girls took off, tempted occasionally by one-of-a-kind wares displayed in shop windows and kiosks.

A dollhouse museum clerk, whose vintage gingham dress reminded Darby of an illustration in her *Little Women* book, collected admission. Their first stop, her favorite from last year, was Prendergast Manor, its decked-out Christmas tree twinkling with lights and tiny ornaments. When Monica pulled them over to a four-story townhouse with a clothing store on the ground floor, Darby sighed at a pint-sized mannequin in a pink satin evening dress topped with a soft white stole draped over its shoulders.

After the girls threaded their way through the exhibits, intent on seeing all they could, Darby rushed into the gift shop. She chose a postcard picture of the pink dress and a greeting card with an illustration of an old-fashioned amusement park.

The clerk examined it closely. "I've never seen this one before. It's got a real vintage feel, doesn't it?"

"Yeah, almost like it's really old," replied Darby. Even the blank insides seemed a bit faded. "It reminds me of someone I know. Hey guys," she called to her pals, "I'll meet you outside."

After paying, she swung around the corner and sat on a shady park bench to go through the cards. Her forehead crinkled as a closer look at the amusement park drawing revealed details she'd missed. *It has a Timeless Voyages ride, like at Mr. Usher's.* She turned it over. Its black text read "Circa 1950." Inside, the blank pages offered nothing.

The card vibrated. *Is there a computer chip somewhere?* Darby held it up to the sunlight, but nothing showed through the thick paper. *Did I imagine that?* It vibrated again in her shaking hands. Lights on the rides began to glow. She tried to read the minute letters on a sign inside the Ferris wheel hub. *Does that say L.U.C.K.?* The sign started flashing on and off. Her mouth dry, she flipped the card open and nearly dropped it.

Now, two words appeared in uneven red print:

Wednesday, midnight!
L.U.

Chapter Ten

JUNE 23

On Wednesday evening in Branch Hall's crafts room, Darby checked the time. *Not even close to midnight.*

The Wild Strawberries were working on a mural canvas, soaking a white sheet in a tub of starchy water. They draped it over two clotheslines, stretching it across the room to dry in the warm night air. While everyone sketched ideas for designs, Darby peered at the clock again. *It's only been two minutes since the last time!* She caught June staring. *Is she reading my thoughts?* Her fingers turned cold. She tried to focus on her half-drawn carousel. *Mr. Usher wouldn't let the twins do that. Would he?*

But June merely pointed to her sister's parrot sketch. Darby sighed with relief. In the end, she voted for the puppies drawn by a cabin mate named Maria, though Jessica's birds won anyway. *The twins are probably mad that I voted against them. But they already don't like me.*

The clock moved five more minutes. *What are Naz and Justin doing right now?* Darby had tracked them down yesterday with her news, enlisting their support to help her warn Mr. Usher about saving his building. They'd planned for tonight. *Everything's set. It couldn't be more perfect.* Except for how time seemed to stand still.

After the girls tacked the stiffened sheet to a wall so they could block out grids for the parrots, Darby returned to her drawing. She sketched a few more lines on the carousel, which sparked a reminder of the orange building. And the children's laughter. *That sound makes Mr. Usher happy. He wants the property filled with kids again.* Her jaw dropped with a brainstorm. *If his son sells the property to Donna for Camp Inch instead of turning it into condos, Mr. Usher will get his wish. He can rest in peace.* As she doggedly counted down the remaining minutes, her resolve to help save the warehouse grew. *I have to make sure he knows.*

When Rochelle finally called it a night and the Wild Strawberries fell into bed, Darby propped herself up against the pillow. Each time her eyes began to close, she snapped awake, then swore she'd just shut them for a second. But by the time Justin tapped on her window, she lay fast asleep.

~∽~

MIDNIGHT...

Outside, the two boys took turns counting on their hands to ten, then fifty, then 100. More time passed. Before long, Justin's watch clicked midnight. He stared at Naz, sharing a thought.

Should we go inside to get her? After weighing the pros and cons, he shook his head.

Naz pulled the paperweight, wrapped in a thick sock, from his pocket. "Might this do something?"

"I don't think so. But let's 'think' her awake."

"Will it work while she sleeps?" Naz asked.

"It better."

Darby, wake up. DARBY, WAKE UP.

Less than a minute later, Darby appeared, her face flushed. "Come on," she whispered. They rushed off, stepping cautiously through the overgrown pathway toward the fieldstone wall.

"The moon isn't as bright as last time," said Justin.

"*Il fait froid.*" Naz shivered, pulling his sweatshirt hood over his head.

Darby fretted, but she breathed a sigh of relief when she spotted the trolley waiting for them beside the ivy-covered gate. "We're here!" She ran ahead, and they all climbed aboard.

Bells clanged, the step folded up, and the firing engines whooshed them airborne. Soon, they were back in the foyer at Carnival King where Mr. Usher motioned them to follow him to the carnival's pulsating lights and ringing sounds.

Darby stopped the boys, whispering, "Now?"

They nodded.

"M-M-Mr. Usher?"

"Yes?"

"W-w-we..." She paused to restart. "We need to tell you something."

"Certainly," he said with a smile, bringing them back to the quiet of his office. "Well?"

Darby took a deep breath. "I heard our camp director say that your son plans to sell your property and build condos, but she wants to buy it instead. S-S-So we wanted you to know about that."

Mr. Usher's smile broadened. "Thank you for conveying this news to me. I'm pleased to learn that she remains interested after all this time. Your concern touches me."

Darby wondered at a glint in his eyes. *Are those tears?*

"I am aware of Geoff's plan, and it must be prevented," he continued. "As it turns out, we have only until August sixth, which is about six weeks away."

"August sixth is the last day of camp," said Naz. "Mamá said she would see me then."

Justin shifted in his seat. "My dad's birthday is August sixth."

"Cool, you can celebrate with him," said Darby, but he just looked away.

"August sixth is my son's deadline. And ours too," added Mr.

Usher, turning to the portrait. "So keep doing your part to make the orange line grow. And on that note, let me do mine. We shall visit Naz's Papá."

~⁂~

"We shall?" Naz's pulse sped up. "But how will we get there? He lives in Morocco."

Mr. Usher pulled out his watch, which flickered as though lit by a candle from within. "All things are possible," he boomed.

With great conviction, Mr. Usher led them into the hall. As they passed under the archway into the carnival's bright lights, he pointed toward Timeless Voyages. "Tonight, we will travel much farther than last time."

Naz rushed toward the swirling crimson, amber, and cobalt blue streamers on Timeless Voyages' blinking sign. He hopped from one foot to the other while Mr. Usher turned a large copper key in the lock of a turnstile.

With a click, the door beyond floated open. Inside, Mr. Usher swept his hand around the circular wood-paneled room, indicating seven curtained doorways. "Your choice, Naz."

Light from the high-domed ceiling's chandelier cast shadows on a rug that hushed Naz's footsteps as he strode forward to recite the words carved above each curtain. "Western Stagecoach. Mirror Maze. Unconventional Flight. Journey to

Mars." His imagination burned with fantastic visions. "The Chambered Nautilus. Mystery Island. Foreign Lands." *Which one will take me home to Papá?* On the verge of choosing, he paused. *If I make a mistake, we might land on another planet.* He spun around for one last look. "I choose Foreign Lands."

With a wink, Mr. Usher pulled open Foreign Lands' amber curtain. He led them down a corridor, lined with travel posters, that ended with three long aisles.

Naz bit his lip while considering his next options: European Landmarks on the left, South American Vistas straight ahead, and Africa Alive to the right.

"I hope Morocco's this way," said Darby, pointing to European Landmarks' illustrations of the Eiffel Tower and Big Ben.

"Morocco is in northern Africa," replied Naz.

"It is?" said Darby. "I had no clue."

Justin admitted, "Me neither."

Veering right toward Africa Alive's ceiling-high display cases, Naz hid a smile at the idea that he knew more geography than his older pals. The first few cases were labelled SUDAN, ETHIOPIA, and KENYA, but he bolted beyond to MOROCCO and pressed his nose as close as he could to its acrylic barrier. Inside, three-dimensional dioramas of architectural ruins and desert landscapes filled him with memories of last year's family vacation.

The next panorama held an ancient fortified city off in the distance. In front, a contemporary metropolis brimming with salmon-pink buildings blazed in a color-streaked sunset that made Naz's chest swell with pride. "This is Marrakech, where I live."

Naz watched Mr. Usher flip his watch open and adjust the dial. As it flickered in the faint illumination, a warm current of air whistled past, while the floor shook like a small earthquake. Crimson, amber, and blue streamers unfurled to the carpeted floor. Darkness fell. Naz's stomach dropped like a falling elevator. He reached for the display case, but it was gone. When he tried to call out, nothing happened. Braced for disaster, he crossed his arms over his head.

After what felt like too long, sunlight replaced the blackout. Naz lowered his arms, finding himself at the corner of an open-air Marrakech market teeming with people. His face lit up. *I'm home.* "We're in the main square," he called to Mr. Usher, Darby, and Justin, nearly drowned out by the noise.

"Stay close," said Mr. Usher.

Naz, followed by the others, took in familiar rows of stalls bearing chickpeas, yellow and green peppers, oranges, bright red tomatoes, purple eggplant, almonds, dates, grilling meats, and spices in every hue. Dodging motorbikes and carts pulled by donkeys, they wound through the aisles. When Darby strayed down a side aisle, Naz yelled, "Watch out!" just in time to prevent her from being knocked over by a speeding bicycle.

"I've never seen this many things to eat in my life," she exclaimed. "What smells so good?"

"Best snails in Morocco," yelled a vendor, offering a platter of white spiral shells.

"Uh, n-n-no." Darby backed away.

Naz guffawed as revulsion distorted her features. He would have lingered at the sight of every dancer and magician, but Mr. Usher marched them away from the din.

"Quickly now," he boomed, heading around a corner and down a few blocks to a domed office building.

Justin pointed at squiggly calligraphy on a sign beside its gold front doors. "What does that mean?"

"It means Ministry of Tourism." Naz's voice rose with excitement. "This way." He tugged open the doors, flew across the patterned tile floor, and clattered up a staircase that curved to a balcony. Running through a keyhole-shaped doorway, he cried, "Papá, I am here."

As Mr. Usher and Darby trailed Naz, Justin sat down on the top stair, dropping his head into his palms.

Darby returned and crouched beside him. "What's wrong?"

"I don't know," he fibbed. *I hope she can't hear me thinking about my father.*

But she simply sat down and hugged her knees to her chest, giggling at the echo her shoes made as she tapped them on the multi-colored tile steps.

Justin re-tied his laces. *I guess it only works if I want it to.*

Darby halted her tapping feet at a 45-degree angle. "Have you figured out how to do all that stuff Mr. Usher said would make the orange line get longer?"

"You mean how we're supposed to bring the stuff we learn at the warehouse back into our lives at camp? And do stuff we don't want to do or don't think we can?"

"Yeah, that. But he also told us he'd give us something we really want. How does he know?"

What I really want, Justin thought, *is to see my dad again, like Naz.* All he said, though, was, "I don't understand that either."

Resuming her shoe tapping, Darby said, "You know what? I bet we'll figure it out. Being friends with you and Naz is a good start."

As he got up, Justin's frown relaxed into a lopsided smile. "It's weird. At home, where everything *seems* normal, I don't feel very good. But with the three of us, where you never know what to expect, like showing up in Africa, I feel better."

Darby followed him through the entryway. "You too, huh?"

~⁂~

Naz waited for Darby and Justin to catch up, then he tiptoed inside an open door. "Papá?" Mr. Usher's reminder that they wouldn't be seen did little to dim his spirits.

Two men, one tall with olive skin and the other fair-haired, talked side by side on a couch. An expanse of windows provided a view of the setting sun, lighting the room in gold.

Naz pointed at the tall man, his eyes glistening. "That is my Papá."

"Erik, this has been an absolutely delightful and productive afternoon," said Papá as the men helped themselves to a platter on the coffee table filled with Naz's favorite lamb canapés.

Would they notice if I took one? Despite his watering mouth, Naz fought the temptation to test Mr. Usher's magical rules.

"I would have invited you to our home this evening," said Papá, "but it's much more comfortable to entertain here since my wife and son have been gone."

"You are hospitable even without the presence of your lovely family," replied Erik, sipping his drink.

"What are they saying?" asked Justin as the conversation continued. "What language is that?"

"Arabic," said Erik, as if in reply.

"*Non, c'est francais*," said Naz, confused. "It is French."

"So," Papá replied, referring to a folder, "you're proposing to hire tour guides who speak French and Arabic to work here with their families for part of the year and in France for the rest?"

"Yes," said Erik. "It's a wonderful opportunity for adventurous souls."

Adventurous souls. Naz remembered his mother's letter. *Like me.* "Oh," he said, raising his hand as if waiting to be called on in class. "We might do that!"

"Do what, young man?" asked Mr. Usher.

"Papá's work is here. Mamá's work is in America. Perhaps we can find a way to live together in two countries at different times, just like he is discussing with this man."

"Indeed," Papá replied, staring in his son's direction.

Naz smiled, his hopes soaring. "Are you speaking to me?"

But Papá continued to address Erik. "I will review our roster for guides with the right qualifications and send you recommendations."

Naz's face crumpled. "I thought he heard me."

"It's too soon to know," said Mr. Usher, fishing the watch from his pocket.

In the blink of an eye, the office darkened with a jolt. Streamers swirled warm wind around. Soon, Naz stood full size before the Marrakech display case, the others nearby. On the way out, he blew a kiss back toward Morocco. "Goodbye, Papá."

"That's all for tonight, my friends," said Mr. Usher. "I will alert you about returning very soon."

As the trolley took off into a sky of fast-moving clouds, Naz pulled the paperweight out of the sock in his pocket. "Look." He displayed it for Darby and Justin to see. "Isn't the orange line different?"

"Yep, it's longer," Justin said. He elbowed Darby. "Remember, earlier tonight, Mr. Usher said he'd better do his part? Well, he did. He gave Naz something he wants, just like he said he would."

"He did?" asked Naz.

"Yeah. He brought you to your dad's office so you could hear him and his friend talking about switching back and forth between two countries, and it made you think of a way to see him more often."

Darby nodded. "That's right."

"*Oui*," said Naz. He wrapped the paperweight in his sock and hugged it to his chest. "That is what I want."

When they landed, thunder in the distance sent them running, and they reached their cabins seconds before the sky opened up with pelting rain.

Chapter Eleven

JUNE 24

Darby tiptoed back into Six South, pausing at the doorway to catch her breath. She made her way across the room, only to stop short at her bed, which she'd left a rumpled mess. Now, it appeared neatly made. She turned slowly. A chill washed over her, as though someone had tossed a bucket of ice water.

From the adjacent bunk, June whispered, "Good morning."

"We waited for you a *very* long time," added Jessica.

"I-I-," she attempted, but the twins snuggled smugly back under their covers.

With trembling hands, Darby pulled back the bedclothes as carefully as she could, praying she wouldn't wake Austine in the bunk below. *They know I've been gone.* A panicky flutter kept her up for what remained of the night. *What am I going to do? What are* they *going to do?*

In the morning, the twins arrived at the bathroom right after Darby finished brushing her teeth. She took a shaky breath. "Are you g-g-going to tell Rochelle?"

They mimicked her question in toothpaste-fueled gibberish then turned their backs.

Fighting waves of nausea, Darby departed. *If they tell the counselors, I won't be able to go to Mr. Usher's ever again.*

~⟞~

More than 100 miles away, Geoff Usher tugged at his hair, stared at the legal brief on his office desk, and reread the same paragraph for the fourth time. His concentration evaporating, he pushed the papers aside.

Why can't I get Katie out of my mind? Was it that dream about when we were kids? Was it really a dream? It seemed so real. She was sitting beside him as he tied his shoelace at the top of a curving tile staircase, hugging her knees to her chest, tapping her shoes on the patterned step. The moment held an intensity that continued to preoccupy him.

Last week, when she looked at him from her garden, he'd almost waved, but she'd turned her back too quickly.

The phone rang. With a wild thought that it might be Katie, he answered it. "Oh, hi, Claire," he said with a sigh at the sound of his secretary's voice. "Yes, please tell him I'll be right there."

~⟞~

Darby managed to eat a few crackers at breakfast, but nothing else looked appetizing. A rain forecast added to her misery.

"No riding today," said Counselor Rochelle. "Pick a few board games from the Game Room and let's head back to the cabin."

Monica recruited Darby, Lindsay, Austine, and Maria to round out a set of Clue players. Grabbing a game token, she said, "I want to be Miss Scarlet."

"So do I," protested Austine.

"Roll for it." Monica shook the dice.

Darby selected Professor Plum, its dark purple marker matching her mood, and the game began. After a few minutes, her attention drifted to the twins' bunk, where Jessica dangled her head and shoulders from the top, whispering to a smirking June.

Ten minutes passed. Austine nudged Darby once. Then twice. "C'mon. It's your turn."

"Oh. Sorry." Tossing the dice, she devised a way to get out of playing so she could be by herself. *And maybe overhear what the twins are saying.* She moved the Professor four spaces into the Billiard Room and ran her eyes around the others' faces as they studied their cards. "I have an Accusation."

"What?" demanded Maria. "Already?"

Unfazed, Darby pretended to consult her Detective Notes, making a check mark with the stubby pencil for authenticity. "It was done by Colonel Mustard in the Billiard Room with a lead pipe." She pulled the cards from the black Solution envelope then hastily pushed them right back in. *Wow, I got two of them right even though I didn't really have a clue.* Amused by her little joke, she feigned frustration at her supposed failure. "Guess I'm out."

While the rest of the players furiously scribbled Detective Notes and carried on without her, Darby headed to her bunk and promptly fell asleep.

She woke as Rochelle asked for everyone's attention. "The Talent Show isn't until the last day of camp," she said, "but we have to plan our performance."

Darby squinted at her watch. *Eleven o'clock... not even lunch time yet. This day is crawling.* She glanced nervously at the twins.

Maria, who had entertained her cabin mates with tales of the year she toured with a road show company of *Annie*, volunteered to explain Talent Show rules. "We did a Rockettes-type dance last year," she began.

Darby groaned and rolled over on her bunk, glowering at the rain. Last year, she helped make costumes. This year she intended something similar. Tuning everything out, her thoughts wandered back to Leroy Usher, Carnival King. Swirling streamers began to float through her head as she drifted off again.

"Darby, that's fabulous!" said Rochelle.

She sat up with a start. Everyone was staring at her. "What is?"

"I love the idea that you're practicing a song to sing for the show."

" *WHAT?* Who told you that?"

"We did." June and Jessica sounded like they'd won a million dollars.

Monica shot Darby a curious look. "That doesn't sound like Darby."

"Oh yes," said Jessica, "she told us that very, very early today."

"You did?" Monica asked.

"I-I-I," stuttered Darby.

June added, "Don't be modest. You were up half the night practicing! Wasn't that what you said when you came back this morning?"

Darby went speechless with horror, as the twins exchanged private chuckles. "I g-g-guess so," she stammered at last, avoiding Monica's wide eyes.

"Well, that's great," said Rochelle. "How about the rest of you dance while Darby sings?"

"I can direct and choreograph the whole number," offered Maria. "It'll be great!"

"Perfect," said Rochelle. As if on cue, the rain stopped, and the sun reappeared. "Look at that. Too late for riding, but we won't miss swimming after all."

June and Jessica smiled sweetly at Darby as they arrived at the Swim Pavilion. She glared back at them, sick to her stomach. When Monica and Lindsay ran off to swim laps in the deep end, she hung behind, floating by herself near the shallow steps and kicking at the water.

Counselor Sally knelt beside her. "You okay?"

"Not really." Darby made a face. "I'm kind of queasy. Can I wait outside on the lawn?"

"All right," said Sally. "We'll catch up when we're done here. Stay nearby, okay?"

Darby climbed out of the pool, tossed on a terry cloth over-suit, and sprinted down the Pavilion's front stairs to the Great Lawn where she flung out her towel.

"Hey, Darby!" Justin, in a nearby circle of his fellow Charging Buffaloes, got up and plopped onto the grass beside her. "I am so tired," he yawned. "How about you?"

"I-I-I…" She choked back tears.

"What's going on?"

"I got caught being out last night by these creepy girls in my c-c-cabin." She explained the twins' plot.

"That's mean," he said with a sympathetic nod, "but it could be worse. They didn't rat you out to your counselor, right?"

"Yeah. But I had to lie about it to my friend Monica," she sniffed, bending sideways to wipe her eyes with her towel.

"Hang on." He ran over to Eugene for some tissues and handed her a few.

"Thank you." She blew her nose, gloom invading her insides. "I don't even know any songs all the way through. Besides, I'll never be able to get up in front of an audience."

"I play the piano. I'll teach you something."

"Really?" Her eyes filled again.

"Hey," he said, grasping her shoulders. "Think of all that happened at Mr. Usher's. Stuff we never could have imagined. This could work out that way too. Remember how he said to try things we don't think we can do?"

"I guess I didn't think of it that way." Darby gave him a weak smile. Spotting her cabin mates on the Swim Pavilion stairs, she scrambled to her feet, gave Justin a hug and ran off calling back, "I hope you're right."

Chapter Twelve

JUNE 25

Despite a rainy forecast, the next day's skies spilled sun over the running track where Counselor Franklin named Justin captain of the Charging Buffaloes' Tournament Day relay team. He led off with a practice lap, his brain buzzing with memories. *It's cool being captain. Like in Little League, when Dad was coach.* He sighed. *But not anymore. Not for a long time.*

More than a year ago, his father's emphysema had gotten worse, and everything changed. Disrupted routines became routine. So did postponed vacations. He winced at the reminder of the agonized coughing that echoed through closed doors. After the doctors had transferred his dad to an Arizona clinic, phone calls eased the anxiety that woke Justin every day, but school prevented visiting. *That was bad enough. Then it got worse.*

At first, the warm, dry climate had improved his father's health. Justin dreamed nightly of a reunion at Thanksgiving, tucking a snapshot of the two of them into the pocket of every outfit he wore. Then a setback cancelled that plan.

Mom travelled back and forth. Even when she stayed with Justin in Milwaukee for Christmas, her work kept her preoccupied. More often than not, he came home to just a housekeeper. The silence at meals had sent him rushing to his piano or to the television for companionship. Soon, he felt almost invisible.

When Mom called one day last April, her broken voice revealed Dad had gone even before she got out the words. He'd slumped to the floor, his throat almost too tight to reply. For the rest of that day, one hope kept him from running away: *I have to see Dad one last time.* Instead, by the time she returned home, ashes inside a fancy urn were all that remained. The funeral, with very little family on either parent's side, came and went quickly.

Afterward, Justin discussed it with no one, not even classmates or baseball pals. *What if I cried in front of everybody?* Sobs from behind his mother's bedroom door triggered a leaden weight in his stomach that kept him quiet, no matter how much he wanted to open up. *Who could I talk to anyway?* Mom seemed too absorbed to pay much attention. *No one listens, so what's the point?* Eventually, it was more natural to simply remain silent all the time.

Justin handed off the baton to Hugh, ran past his teammates, and dropped to the grass by himself. Before long, Naz jogged over

"We lost our Tug-Of-War game, but it was great fun," he

said, brushing a towel on his mud-caked shorts and legs. "Have you concluded your race?"

"Not yet." Justin wiped his eyes with his sleeve. "We're practicing."

"Are you *triste?*"

"I'm not crying, if that's what you think." When Naz shook his head, Justin said, "Okay, what does it mean?"

Naz translated.

Yeah. I am *sad. Despondent,* thought Justin, using the term he'd overheard the doctor telling his mom. As he rubbed his eyes, Mr. Usher's promise ran through his mind. *Help yourself by doing something you don't want to do, or something you don't think you can.* He held his breath. *Naz might listen.* Without waiting to decide whether he would, or he wouldn't, Justin plunged ahead. "I was thinking about my father. He, um... he died last April."

Naz gasped. "What happened?"

"He had emphysema."

"What is that?"

"It's in your lungs and makes it hard to breathe." Without looking up, he added, "He was far away, so I never got to say goodbye."

"That *is* very sad. I am..." He paused. "*Désolé,*" was all he could manage.

"If that means 'sorry,' thanks."

"When I miss Grandpapá, Mamá reminds me that he survives inside me," said Naz, touching his chest. He jumped at a blast from Rich's whistle. "I must depart."

"Wait. Did you hide the orange paperweight?"

"*Oui.* It is secure in my trunk. *Au revoir pour le moment.*"

"Ah rah vwar, Naz." As Justin watched him go, a ripple of relief began loosening the knot that had confined him for so long.

By the end of Tournament Day, the Charging Buffaloes' four gold medals hung from red ribbons on the bulletin board next to Justin's window. While the others relived their athletic feats on the steps, he dressed for bed.

Eugene stuck his head inside the door. "C'mon out."

"No thanks." Justin lay back on his bunk.

"Want me to stay here and talk?"

"About what?"

"Stuff. We could tell jokes."

Justin feigned a yawn. His bunkmate didn't weird him out as much. He just wasn't ready to break the habit that kept him more comfortable alone. Then a jolt ran through him, and he sat straight up. *Remember this afternoon? Help yourself by doing something you don't want to do.* He turned to Eugene. "Whadda you got?"

"Um… let me see. What did one eye say to the other eye?"

"What?"

"Don't look now, but something between us smells."

Justin grimaced. "I got one, although it's not really a joke. Did you notice how our counselors' names are Ben and Franklin, like the historic guy?"

Eugene's eyes lit up. "Yeah, I've read a bunch of books about him. He's from Massachusetts, like me. I went to his birthplace with my cousins last fall."

"What's there?" asked Justin.

"Well, nothing except a bust of him on the building that's there now."

"That much?" Justin laughed. He jumped down from his bunk and opened his footlocker. "I go to a school named after him," he said, pulling out a T-shirt.

"Wow," said Eugene, squinting at Benjamin Franklin's image under the school's emblem. "Can I show this to the other guys?"

"Why would they care?"

"Trust me," Eugene said, heading outside.

"Whatever." Justin turned off the cabin lights, crawled into bed and stared out at the midnight blue sky. The bulletin board's medals, lit by moonlight, caught his eye. One of them looked especially shiny. He lifted it off the tack. It glimmered in his hand as two red lines gradually faded in over the Camp Inch logo:

Monday!
L.U.

Chapter Thirteen

JUNE 26

The next morning, Justin somehow missed Darby and Naz at breakfast, but he located her in the mail room pulling some papers from an oversized manila mailer.

"Hey, guess what?" he said, taking a letter from the clerk. "I got a message about Monday..."

"Ooh, my dad sent me some of his drawings." She glanced up as he stuffed his envelope in his pocket. "Don't you want to check and see if your parents sent you anything?"

"My parents?" Justin asked, as if she'd called them extraterrestrials. Mr. Usher's summons temporarily forgotten, he concentrated on his shoes. *Should I tell her about my dad? It helped to tell Naz, even when I didn't want to.* He took a deep breath and met her eyes. "The letter is from my mom. My father died in April."

"What? How?" She hid her head in her hands. "I mean I'm sorry. That's awful."

After Darby heard Justin's story, she blinked away tears and looked down at her dad's drawings. He didn't have to read her mind to recognize the gratitude that spread across her face.

Before they parted, Justin filled her in about Mr. Usher. A bit later, when Naz and his cabin mates were about to enter Branch Hall, Justin pulled him aside to catch him up too.

"*Superbe*," said Naz, then he whispered, "The orange line got longer last night."

"It did? Why?"

"I don't know."

On his way back to Eight North, Justin stopped short. *I know! Mr. Usher told us to help ourselves by doing something we'd rather not. Like I did yesterday with Naz and Eugene. And just now with Darby. I can't wait to tell him.*

~⁂~

MIDNIGHT... TWO DAYS LATER

As Justin passed under the archway into the carnival, which rang with calliope music and shone as bright as a summer afternoon, he had his chance.

"Excellent," Mr. Usher responded. "You have been making progress at camp. Equally important," he added, nodding at Naz and Darby, "when you join me here, you all affect matters yet to come." He inserted Timeless Voyages' turnstile key. "Justin, tonight you choose our destination."

Justin studied the circular room's seven doorways, ablaze with resolve to make Mr. Usher's "matters yet to come" work out, whatever they were. *Journey to Mars sounds good. But what about Mystery Island?* Finally, enticed by Mirror Maze's possibilities, he pointed to its crimson curtain, and Mr. Usher pulled it aside.

They entered a narrow corridor lined on both sides by full-length mirrors and illuminated by blue-tinged lights that gave their bodies an eerie glow. In one of the reflections, Justin caught Mr. Usher's eye, the watch ticking in his hand.

The corridor ended with two choices. Justin picked the left one, only to be confronted with new options. This time, he went right, but they wound up at a dead end. Mirrors reflected Justin's red checked shirt everywhere he turned.

Naz twisted around. "Six, seven, eight, nine…"

"What are you doing?"

"Counting every red checked shirt."

"You'd need a computer to calculate it…" Justin trailed off. Red checks washed away to blackness; then dark space faded into light. In the panel straight ahead, Justin identified his bedroom where he – or someone very much like him – typed furiously on a computer keyboard.

"What are you writing?" asked Naz.

Justin bent forward. "Not sure. I could read it with binoculars." Just like that, the bedroom blurred. When the image sharpened into focus, "Mirror Justin" stood on a mountainside, binoculars at the ready.

Darby chuckled.

"The mirror shows what I'm saying," Justin marveled.

Mr. Usher nodded. "Try it again."

"Justin Pennington, piano soloist," he exclaimed, his imagination fired. Decked out in a tux with tails, "Mirror Justin" seated himself at a large Steinway surrounded by an orchestra.

Quick, something else. "Sheriff. Cowboy. Sky diver. Navy Seal. Jet pilot." His reflection changed uniforms as fast as the words left his lips. "Astronaut," he whooped, admiring "Mirror Justin" floating in zero gravity with a blue planet circling beneath.

Darby and Naz applauded.

"Senator. President. King!" Justin lit up at the sight of his throne, but he scowled at the royal robe. "It's so big. I look like a shrimp. Wait – oh no!" Justin's kingdom dissolved into an underwater scene crawling with shellfish.

The others laughed, while Mr. Usher hid a smile. "All right, settle down. There's more here than games. Look deeply. What do you want most of all?"

"Anything?" he asked, his eyes reddening. "Even like seeing my Dad?"

"Everything."

Justin curled his fingers into fists and concentrated on the mirror. "Baseball. With Dad."

The boy in the mirror ran to catch a batted ball from a tall man, his sandy hair glinting in the daylight. Justin gazed wistfully at his dad's vitality, barely remembering him like this. "Okay, Christmas. Three years ago."

Mom and Dad materialized, almost like in a home video, helping his nine-year-old self rip off holiday wrapping from a blue bicycle. Their happiness crushed the air out of him. *Too much.* He brushed away tears. "More recent."

This time, Dad, his skin ashen, seemed big as life, reading what looked like a doctor's chart in an unfamiliar white room. Justin backed up in surprise, his fists still clenched.

Dad wrapped the ties of his robe and got up to greet a visitor, whose white jacket bore an embroidered name over the chest pocket. The man shook his head, pointing at some numbers on the medical chart. When he departed, Dad's sober expression deepened.

Then the mirror shimmered with golden light. Dad came toward him.

Shaking in expectation, Justin breathed in what smelled like a long-forgotten aftershave. He uncurled his fingers, pressing his hands and face against the glass, as if he might push through. "Can you hear me?"

Familiar hands grasped Justin's. *Woah.*

"I love you, son." His father's voice parked itself in Justin's heart.

"I love you too."

"It's time for goodbye."

"No." Stifling a sob, he vowed never to let go. Only when cold glass replaced warm flesh on his palms did his grip loosen. All that remained in the mirror was the reflection of Justin and his red checked shirt. "Bye, Dad."

Darby's hand flew to her mouth, and Naz pressed his palms onto the top of his head. In the background, Mr. Usher's watch disappeared into a deep pocket.

Still shaking as they boarded the trolley, Justin whispered, "Thank you."

"I thank you," replied Mr. Usher. "Keep doing your parts. If we all do so, progress will be made in ways you could never imagine."

Chapter Fourteen

JUNE 29

Dear Darby,

Dad and I enjoyed your letter and descriptions of the dollhouses. We're very impressed with all that you're doing. Keep it up!

One of my clients is opening a restaurant, and I'm putting together their ad campaign. Your father has several galleries that want to see his new work, especially the painting he made from the sketches we sent you.

I ran into Mrs. Thig at a luncheon last week. She is looking forward to your return and asked that I remind you to avoid picking up any poor habits while you're riding Western at camp. I might speak with the camp director about offering English-trained horses for girls like you who study formally.

Time for my cooking class. Dad will write tomorrow.

Mom

P.S. Be sure to wash your clothes regularly.

Darby sat cross-legged on a Branch Hall rocking chair, shaking her head over her mother's Western saddle warning. *I knew she'd lose it over that.* She couldn't even imagine Mom's reaction to news that her daughter hadn't washed a scrap of clothing in the last week and a half.

Naz rushed up the stairs clutching a white sock. "Look," he whispered, climbing into the chair next to hers, "the orange line became longer last night." He pulled out the paperweight, and they put their heads together.

"Awesome," she whispered back. "Almost halfway. I wonder when Mr. Usher will invite us to come back."

"I feel sure he will alert us very soon."

A few calliope strains burst past their ears.

Darby laughed. "That confirms it." Staring at the billowing clouds, she envisioned her turn to choose a Timeless Voyages adventure, almost certain she'd decide on the Chambered Nautilus. "I can't wait."

～∽～

"Where's Eugene?"

"I don't know," Kenny replied. "Who cares?"

"He's still inside looking for something," said Harper.

Justin left his cabin mates on their way to the Swim Pavilion after dinner and ran back inside Eight North, finding his bunkmate flinging clothes onto his mattress.

"I can't go," he mumbled. "My swimsuit's in my laundry bag."

"Wear it anyway." Justin suppressed a sigh.

"Wear it anyway?" Eugene exclaimed. "No, that's not an option."

This time, Justin laughed at his friend's fussiness, but he tossed him an extra pair of his own trunks, and they reached the Swim Pavilion in time for Franklin's explanation of the rules for Pool Soccer.

Hoisting the largest watermelon Justin had ever seen, the counselor said. "It's like soccer, only in the shallow end of the pool. First team to get this thing to the opposing wall wins. And," he added, "you have to use your feet to move it. No hands or arms."

Counselor Ben separated the Charging Buffaloes into two groups, so Justin gathered Harper, Eugene, Hugh, and Emmanuel for a strategy meeting, suggesting they each block one of the opposing players.

With a blast from Franklin's referee whistle, the cabin mates took turns pushing the watermelon close to their opponents' wall. "Get out of my way," Kenny yelled.

"I will after we win." Justin managed to kick the watermelon back to the center. Before Kenny noticed, he'd maneuvered it several feet toward his team's goal.

"Get him!" Kenny attempted to block Justin, knocking him over with his elbow.

"Penalty on Kenny," signaled Franklin. "I said no arms. You're out for a minute."

When Justin smirked, Kenny swatted water at Justin, who swatted back.

The melon made several trips back and forth, nearly falling into the deep end, but Eugene lunged under to drive it away, ingesting gulps of water in the process. Eventually, Justin's kick secured the victory and his teammates carried him back to the cabin, hooting and yelping.

"What'd you get?" scoffed Kenny. "Nothing."

"Bragging rights," retorted Harper, leading his winning teammates onto Eight North's porch.

While they toasted their victory with hot cocoa, Justin took his inside and climbed onto his bunk.

"Hey, Pennington, get out here!" hollered Hugh.

"Nah, I'm good."

"C'mon. Without you, we would've been toast."

For a moment, Justin remained still. But by now, he'd almost gotten used to trying things he didn't want to do. "Okay, okay." Climbing down, he grabbed his hot chocolate. Its warmth, which felt like his dad's palms, spread through him. He talked with the guys till bedtime, his outlook growing brighter than a noonday sun.

Chapter Fifteen

JUNE 30

Chad Usher took more than a week to get in touch with his sister, the time spent racking his brain for the perfect approach. In the end, on Wednesday morning, he simply left her a voicemail, then drummed his fingers on his kitchen counter. His gaze never left the phone. When it rang a few seconds later, he grabbed the handset. "Katie?"

"Chad?"

After an awkward silence, he cleared his throat. "Thanks for calling back."

More silence.

"Are you all right?" she asked.

Her tense tone cautioned him to tread carefully. "Yes. I'm happy it's you."

"It has been a long time."

"I think so too. Will you meet me at Pop's warehouse tomorrow?"

She didn't reply right away. "We've been through this. Do you have any new ideas?"

"I don't know," he said. "I found something important there, and I'd like to show it to you."

After another brief silence, Katie replied, "Okay. Twelve noon?"

"Twelve noon," he said. "Thanks, I'll see you then."

When Rich's Rangers returned to their cabin after lunch, Naz checked the paperweight, but the orange line hadn't changed since he'd shown it to Darby yesterday.

"Guys," said Counselor Woody, "Rich wants us to take a quiz while he's at a counselor's meeting."

"Like school?" asked Odell, his face incredulous.

To disguise his love of school quizzes, Naz joined in the grumbling.

"Well," sighed Woody, passing out paper and pencils, "let's see if we can make it, uh, entertaining." He scanned Rich's question sheet. "Okay, write down the names of five Presidents. First one to finish, raise your hand for a prize."

"What's the prize?" asked Wilson.

"Money." Woody jingled some coins in his pocket. "Get going."

Naz looked around. His was the only still pencil.

Brough's hand shot up first, and he read his list. "Lincoln, Washington, Roosevelt, Jefferson, Roosevelt."

"You said Roosevelt twice," Naz observed.

"Don't you know there's two Presidents with that name?" said Brough, noticing Naz's blank paper. "You didn't even get any."

"I have little knowledge of American history," he replied.

"Who's the head of Morocco, Naz?" asked Woody, tossing Brough a quarter.

"Our king," Naz said.

"Cool," exclaimed Charlie. "Does he wear a suit of armor?"

After Woody translated into French, Naz laughed. "No, he wears a *costume d'affaires.*"

"That means business suit," Woody translated. "Tell us more, Naz."

"At a special occasion," Naz continued, stopping every so often for help with a word from the counselor, "he wears a traditional robe called a djellaba." He pulled out his photo album to show the boys a picture of his father dressed in a loose flowing gown with full sleeves and a head cover. "Like this. Perhaps even more decorated."

"Don't you trip when you walk?" asked Odell, turning the pages to see all Naz's photos. "Hey, you're playing soccer."

"Tout le monde joue au fútbol."

Woody translated, "Everyone plays soccer. Although," he added, "it's called football everywhere except the U.S."

"I thought you were from France," said Charlie. "You speak

French."

Freed by Rich's absence, Woody translated while Naz explained that in Morocco most people speak French or Arabic. "But my country has at least seven languages."

"Really? Do you get to pick which one?"

"Not really," Naz replied. "It depends where you live."

"What about movies?" Wilson asked. "Did you ever see *Star Wars* or *Return of the Jedi*?"

"*Bien sûr.*" Naz transfixed the boys with revelations that some of the epic series was filmed in Morocco. "You can still visit the structures they built for the film, and you can take a tour. They look like big ruins..." He stopped abruptly when Rich returned and stared suspiciously at the silent group.

"How'd you do on the quiz?"

"Ah," said Woody with a wink to the boys. "We started but we got sidetracked by a very educational culture lesson."

"It's time to write letters home anyway."

"Again?" Charlie groaned. "We already did that."

"More than a week ago," said Rich. "Up and at 'em!"

"Who is Adam?" Naz whispered to Woody. Careful to avoid Rich's ire, he'd switched back to English.

"Adam? What Adam, Naz?"

"Up and Adam, what does that mean?"

Woody laughed. "It's an expression. He's not saying 'Adam.'

He's saying 'at 'em,' like 'at them.'"

"Who?" asked Naz.

"What?"

"Perhaps I will never speak English very well," complained Naz.

"You're doing fine. When you got here, you could barely pronounce Milwaukee." Woody shooed him off, starting a letter home. "Go on, get going on yours."

Naz climbed up onto his bunk to write Papá, describing his cabin mates' interest in Morocco and news of the upcoming square dance. *What else?* He doodled on the paper. Mr. Usher's reminder drifted through his mind. *Everything you experience here is of little value unless you bring it back into your lives.* After replaying his adventures at the warehouse, he began scribbling furiously.

Will you come to live with us here in America for part of the year? Then may we live with you at home during the rest of the time? Would it not be wonderful to be together no matter where we live? I miss you very much. Please, Papá, please do consider my suggestion.

Naz turned his back on the others and crossed his fingers. Diving into the protective sock, he unrolled the paperweight from within. The orange line had moved slightly. But enough to reach the halfway mark. *Yes!* Disguising his glee with a frown, he stashed the paperweight in his trunk and returned to Papá's letter.

As he finished writing out the address on the envelope, his eyes widened at a funny mark in the corner that hadn't been there before. In very small red type, it said,

Thursday
12 noon
L.U.

~⌘~

The Wild Strawberries dressed up for square dancing, several sporting mascara and lipstick, including Darby, who'd readily accepted when Maria offered to share hers. She checked her face in the bathroom mirror, entranced at the almost grownup staring back. *My mom would flip out.* She gave her reflection a wicked grin. *But she'll never know.*

When the cabin mates arrived at Branch Hall, June and Jessica ran their hands through tinsel that decorated the staircase banister, nearly dislodging a sign spelling out "Country Cotillion" in shiny green and white metallic letters. Darby shook her head, joining Monica and Lindsay at the dessert-filled refreshment station. As they "oohed" and "ahhed" at the silver, white, and gold balloons floating on the ceiling, the room filled with other campers.

"Do you know how to air-squay ance-day?" asked Lindsay.

"Oh-nay," said Darby, but Monica told them "They're supposed to each-tay us."

"Okay, folks. I believe we're ready," announced "Cowboy Bob," also known as camp's Assistant Director McKendrick. He struck up his fiddle, and Activities Manager Abby Pearson demonstrated the steps, her crisp petticoats swooshing dramatically every time she swung around.

In less than twenty minutes, Cowboy Bob had Darby, Monica, Lindsay, and the other fledgling dancers attempting complex combinations.

"All aboard," he called, his bow flying back and forth, "it's heel and a toe..."

"Swing your partner, do-si-do...

Pass thru, wheel thru, right and left grand...

Chain 'em back with your left hand...

Bow to your neighbor, allemande right...

Get back home, and swing tonight...

Ace of diamonds, jack of spades...

Meet your partner, all promenade!"

As campers clapped, stamped, and twisted to the infectious rhythms, Branch Hall blazed with their exuberance.

At the halfway break, Darby caught her breath at the table

labelled Cactus Cocktails. Sipping from an exotic barrel-shaped vessel, she laughed. "It's just fruit juice."

"What did you expect?" mocked Jessica. "Beer?"

June cackled.

"It... it... it's..."

Naz hurried over, interrupting her retort.

"I must speak with you and Justin," he said, grabbing dessert from a platter marked Do-Si-Donuts.

"He's not here," said Darby, glaring back at the twins. "What's up?"

Naz paused, staring at her eyes and mouth. "You are different."

"Did I smear my lipstick?" she worried, but Naz's news concerned Mr. Usher.

"He contacted me!"

"What did he say?" When the fiddle struck back up, Darby pulled Naz into her dance circle.

"Shoot for the moon..." called Cowboy Bob.

In time with the music, Naz told her, "Thursday at noon."

"Hand over hand... Heel and a toe..."

Lines of boys and girls threaded into each other, sweeping Darby forward.

"Allemande thar... Bow to your beau."

She stomped her foot in frustration. "We have to wait.

Later."

Afterward, Darby caught up with Naz.

"Tomorrow at noon," he repeated.

"Noon?" she cried. "How are we going to get away?"

He shrugged. "*Je ne sais pas.*"

"Justin might have an idea," she said. "Let's find him at breakfast."

~~∽~~

JULY 1

But the next morning, the Charging Buffaloes' table remained unoccupied.

"They're on an overnight," McKendrick told Darby, "at Paradise Picnic Grounds across the lake."

Her stomach sinking, she waited for Naz to finish breakfast, tapping her shoes impatiently on Branch Hall's front steps. *Wait a minute. Paradise Picnic Grounds – that's how I got to L.U.C.K.'s horseshoes the first time. Maybe Justin can go that way and meet us there.*

Darby grabbed Naz as soon as Rich's Rangers filtered out of Branch Hall's front door. "Justin's at the campgrounds on the other side of the orange building."

"How will he know of my summons from Mr. Usher?" he asked, occupied with a sizable burrito.

"I don't know, and it's already ten o'clock," she said. "Do you think it would work to 'think' him a message that he should get to L.U.C.K. the same way I did the first time I went?"

"Perhaps. But how will *we* arrive there?"

"Good question," she said. "We can't just sneak off to the trolley in broad daylight."

As Naz tore open a sugar packet, pouring it onto his burrito and taking a bite, Darby blanched. "You're going to make yourself sick." Then she brightened. "Hey, *that's* it! Get it?"

He shook his head, his mouth too full to reply.

"We can get away from our groups by pretending we're sick. Our counselors will send us to the infirmary," she explained. "Get it now?"

Naz swallowed. "Yes," he said. "No," he added. "I am not sure," he concluded.

"Listen. The nurses probably don't watch you all the time in the infirmary. When they take a break, we'll leave them a note saying we feel better. Then, instead of going back to our cabins, we'll go to the wall."

Naz hesitated. "Mamá would not want me to tell a fib. But," he said after swallowing another chunk of burrito, "I cannot miss an adventure to help Mr. Usher. *D'accord.*"

"That means yes, right?"

He nodded.

"Great, meet me at the infirmary in a half hour or so?"

"Yes," he replied and started down the stairs.

WAIT! The message to Justin. Darby held out her hand, Naz took it, and she concentrated. *Today, Leroy Usher, Carnival King. Twelve noon.* She did her best with the complex instructions, concluding with, *keep an eye out for the sign that says Private Property.*

It has to work," she affirmed. "It's our only chance!"

Chapter Sixteen

Across the lake, Justin stretched and yawned as he helped the counselors flip bacon strips sizzling over the campfire. None of the Charging Buffaloes had gotten much sleep last night, what with Ben's ghost stories. He eyed the trees, so ominous in the dark but harmless now, then checked his watch. *No wonder I'm super hungry. It's after 10.* This morning's epic "world's best second baseman" debate had delayed breakfast.

While Franklin and Ben doused the fire, Justin delivered bacon to cabin mates at the picnic table and filled his plate. "Last batch, guys."

"I'm sick of all this fatty food," said Eugene. "Why can't we have something healthier? Like tofu."

"Eww," groaned Hugh.

"Tofu?" jeered Emmanuel. "That's gross."

"You're gross," countered Eugene distastefully.

"*You're* gross," yelled Kenny, throwing a roll in Eugene's direction.

"Don't you know better than to waste your food?" Eugene turned to Justin. "You've heard of tofu, haven't you?"

"Yes, but I've never eaten it." *And I never will.* "I love bacon and eggs, especially how they smell." He bent over his food, inhaling with great expectations. "Huh?"

"What?" said Eugene.

"Smell this. It doesn't smell like bacon, does it?" said Justin.

Eugene wrinkled his nose. "I'm not smelling that."

"It smells like cotton can..." Justin stopped, wiping away sweat that had broken out on his forehead.

Eugene scurried off toward the circle of sleeping bags to tidy up his belongings, while Justin sniffed again. *I know that cotton candy smell means something,* he thought, more uneasy than he'd been for weeks, *but what?*

After Katie Usher rushed through her grocery shopping, she started off for Leroy Usher, Carnival King. Sun blazing through the windshield warmed her face, and the great expanse of road ahead promised a welcome reunion. *I've missed my brothers. There's been too much silence between us.*

Preoccupied with the possibilities of what Chad had found that he couldn't discuss on the phone, she circled White Falls Highway's exit onto the thoroughfare. Then she pulled over beside the totem pole at the road's edge exactly like Dad used to do so she and her brothers could see it.

Memories of their visits to L.U.C.K. flooded back: wandering the aisles playing hide and seek... posing in the funny mirrors… their carousel horses. She leaned against the steering wheel, an ache filling her chest at the unkind words they'd hurled at each other last time they were there months ago.

From between the trees, children's voices softly filtered out. The totem pole shined fleetingly with a golden glow. Her head snapped up. *What's moving in there?* But now the pole looked as it always did, quiet and still. She shook it off and drove away, glancing uncertainly in the rearview mirror. *Must have been my imagination.*

Justin raced to roll up his sleeping bag, crumple his belongings into a duffel bag, and pick up trash, as eager as his cabin mates to begin the group's scavenger hunt.

By eleven o'clock, the picnic grounds bore no obvious signs of the Charging Buffaloes' rowdy camp-out, and Counselor Ben divided the boys into two teams. "There's fifteen items on your lists. Whichever group finds the most stuff wins one of these." He produced a one-dollar bill. "Each."

"Where are we supposed to get a bird's feather?" asked Emmanuel.

"*Not* off a live bird," warned Counselor Franklin. "This stuff is all around here." He handed a burlap collection bag to each team. "Be back no later than twelve thirty."

While Justin and his teammates studied the list, Hugh asked,

"Can I be captain? I have a compass," he added, brandishing his versatile flashlight.

The boys exchanged blank looks, but Justin said, "Sure."

"Okay, suckers, this way." Hugh led them past an arrow-shaped sign reading INLAND ROUTE BACK TO CAMP INCH etched in white letters. He spotted a pinecone right off. "Anyone have something to cross it out?"

"Doesn't your flashlight have one?" joked Harper, using his pen to make the first check mark on the card.

Over the next forty-five minutes, the fivesome straggled down the path, eyes scouring the ground. A black stone showed up next, followed by a bird feather, acorn, piece of paper, penny, purple wildflower, a Y-shaped twig, and ten pine needles, all carefully laid in the collection bag. "We're doing really good," said Emmanuel. "I bet the other guys won't find stuff like this."

Ahead, a signpost caught Justin's attention. He leaned against it to rest then jumped off and twisted around. CAMP INCH VIA WHITE FALLS HIGHWAY: ¼ MILE EAST, it said, pointing left. PRIVATE PROPERTY! pointed right. Something gnawed at his brain. *But what?* He held his breath, as if waiting for a sneeze to arrive.

When Hugh led them to the right, Justin kept his mouth shut, private property or not.

Harper studied the card. "We don't have sunflower seeds, a

leaf that's not green, a piece of rope..."

"Hey, what's that?" interrupted Emmanuel, squinting off in the distance. "What does it say on that building? L. U. C. K.," he spelled. "Luck?"

Justin's heart pounded. The road ahead led to Mr. Usher's warehouse, standing no more than 100 yards away, its corner turrets jutting up over the fieldstone wall.

"Maybe it's a prison," said Hugh. "Wouldn't it be cool if we saw a guy in chains?"

"No," scoffed Harper. "Why would it say 'luck' if it was a prison?"

"I don't think it's anything," said Justin. "This road hasn't been used very often."

"Well, what's that then?" demanded Hugh at the sound of an approaching pickup truck, which slowed beside the boys.

"Hello, kids," said the driver, a dark-skinned man who stared at Justin from incongruously blue eyes.

Like Naz's. Justin struggled to figure out why the man seemed familiar.

"What're you doing out here?"

"We're on a scavenger hunt," said Emmanuel.

"Is that right?" The man smiled.

"Mister," asked Hugh, handing over his list, "do you have any of the stuff that isn't checked off?"

"Bingo," he replied, tossing them a half-eaten bag of sunflower seeds. "But nothing else, sorry!"

"Hey, thanks!"

"Are you boys from Camp Inch?"

"Yeah," said Emmanuel.

"That's not a prison, is it?" asked Harper, pointing to the orange building.

"No, that's my family's warehouse," the man replied. "Your camp's been our neighbor for years."

"Of course!" said Justin before he could stop himself. He grinned broadly. *It's Mr. Usher's son.*

The man peered at him again. "I gotta go. You boys be careful and stay off this road."

Justin checked his watch. *Coming up on noon.* He stared after the truck. *Now the cotton candy smell makes sense.* "Hey," he said, "let's split up and meet back here in half an hour. That'll give us a better chance of finding the rest of the stuff. We can synchronize our watches."

"I don't have a watch." Hugh bristled.

"Just come with me," said Emmanuel.

As they went off in different directions, Justin surrendered to the forces pulling him toward Leroy Usher, Carnival King.

Chapter Seventeen

At Camp Inch's archery range, which lay on the property's easternmost edge behind the administration building, Rich's Rangers set up ten targets, lugging them by their round white foam sections. As they arranged the wooden legs on a line marked fifteen yards from the firing point, Counselor Rich pulled out bows and arrows from a small shed. He directed the Rangers into single file and launched an instruction drill that left Naz plenty of time to go over his plan for escape to the infirmary.

Eventually, Counselor Woody pointed to his watch. Rich, grabbing Odell's shoulders to straighten his posture, concluded with a stern reminder to look right down the arrow for a good aim. "Do you understand?" he asked.

At the far end of the line of fidgeting boys, Charlie whispered, "*Oui,*" to Naz.

Rich whirled around, glaring. "What did you say?"

"We said we understand," answered Charlie with a straight face, but Naz covered his mouth to hide a grin.

While the counselors distributed equipment, Naz examined his arrow's stiff feathers, which matched the yellow, red, and blue circles surrounding the target's black center dot. He ran his fingers over the bow's smooth wood, picturing himself drawing it and shooting a bull's eye. If he left now, he'd miss out. Second thoughts about Darby's plan filtered through his head. *But I promised.* He gave the bow one last look. *Ah, je dois... I must.* With a dramatic flourish, he dropped the bow and arrow, doubled over, and grabbed his stomach as if in great pain.

Rich remained busy appraising other campers' stances, but Woody ran to him. "What's wrong?"

"*Je suis...*" he began, then flinched and switched to English. "I am sick. I feel I will throw out," he said, kneeling for extra effect.

"Uh oh." Woody placed his hand on Naz's forehead, signaling to Odell. "Take Naz to the infirmary. It's right over there," he said, indicating the administration building. "Make sure he sees the nurse, then come right back."

Odell helped Naz to his feet, holding him by the shoulders as Naz tried his best to stagger off.

~⸻~

The eight-bed infirmary occupied rooms in the administrative building, leaving Darby and Naz about as far from Camp Inch's west end as they could be. But that obstacle paled beside Nurse Louise's immovable presence, which brought Darby close to panic.

"There's no temperature, dear. But you're flushed, and your heart rate is elevated. You'll need to rest here."

"Maybe I should go back to my cabin." Darby eyed the round clock on the canary-yellow wall above the doctor's office scale. It read eleven thirty. She and Naz would need to leave immediately to make it before noon.

"Oh, no," soothed the nurse, firmly guiding her onto the gray-blanketed, metal-frame cot. "If you have something contagious, we don't want to take a chance. I'll check your temperature again in a bit. Be back soon."

After she left, Darby went over to the white-curtained window, attempting to raise it, but it seemed stuck. She gazed fretfully at the trees outside as she listened to Nurse Louise greeting Naz in the room next door.

"Well, young man," she said, "Are you still feeling nauseous?"

"Yes, I think I am," he said. "Perhaps mixing sugar in my burrito was a mistake."

Darby rolled her eyes. *So was my idea about coming here.* She checked the time again then lay on her cot, head propped up on her hand, her face glum.

Next door, Naz continued, "I have to go."

"Around the corner," replied Nurse Louise.

Darby heard her pour a glass of water. A spoon clinked

when she mixed something into it.

Naz stuck his head inside Darby's room. "She said I can go," he whispered.

"No," Darby sighed, rolling onto her back. "She meant you could go to the bathroom. Basically, we're trapped."

Chad's newly made key released L.U.C.K.'s entrance padlock with a click. He pushed open both sides of the wrought-iron gate, enjoying the warehouse's sunlit radiance, then returned to his truck and parked next to the wooden doors.

Inside, silence reigned. Whistling softly, he wandered into the foyer. Light streaming in from high windows illuminated dust particles dancing over the crates and stacks. He unlocked his father's office and flipped on the light, fishing in his pocket for another bag of sunflower seeds. *Nope.* The scavenger hunt boys got the only one he had. He studied the family portrait, struck by how much young Geoff reminded him of that kid he'd just seen.

His watch beeped, marking 12 noon. *Will Katie be late? Will she come at all?* He rubbed his chin. *It was yesterday we talked. She won't forget.* Katie held top honors for reliability in Usher family lore. None of his teenage scrapes proved too complicated for her to untangle. She opened her house for Thanksgiving and Christmas dinners. Throughout the last decade, he and his buddies spent every Sunday at her popcorn/movie get togethers. *Until earlier this year.*

A slamming car door sent him hurrying outside.

Katie, her long brown hair blowing in the breeze, looked up at the bright green L.U.C.K. letters, which matched the color of her vest.

"Over here," called Chad from the doorway.

She turned, her expression betraying an apprehension he understood only too well. They stood silent until she tossed him a few candy bars from her tote bag.

"Milky Ways." *I should have known she'd remember my favorite.* He stood aside to let her into the foyer, her reserve suppressing his instinct to give her a hug. "Thanks for coming."

"What did you want to show me?"

Chad led her to the fun-house mirror where their distorted reflection stretched his blue jeans twice their length and blew up her slim figure like a balloon with feet.

"You look like Jack Sprat, but I look like Miss Piggy," said Katie, switching places. "Much better." She perched on a nearby crate. "So?"

He cleared his throat. "I know it sounds crazy, but when I came here a week and a half ago, Geoff, you, and I were in this mirror. Like when we were kids, riding our carousel horses."

"You mean a photo?"

"Not a photo. More like a movie." He sat next to her. "There were sounds too. Carousel music and children's voices."

Katie's eyebrows rose skeptically. "How could that..." She stopped. "Children's voices?" She shook, as if a chill ran through her.

"What?"

"When I drove by the totem pole earlier, I thought I heard kids' laughter in the trees, but it must have been my imagination. Right?" She got up and squinted into the mirror. "See? It's just you and me," she said with a shrug.

"No," he replied. "Check now."

In the dim depth, a boy wearing a red checked shirt pressed his hands against the inside of the glass, his eyes full of tears. Nearby stood a girl, her palms over her mouth, and a shorter boy, his hands on the top of his head, their images curved and elongated,

"Look at us," she said, her face white. "Why were we so sad?"

Within seconds, the children vanished.

"I don't know," he said. "Did they somehow find out we haven't spoken for months?"

Katie met his words with a brief silence. "I'm sorry about our argument," she finally replied. "I was wrong to say the things I said, to let this go on for so long."

"I'm sorry too," he said, his voice filled with relief.

As they went to hug each other, a burst of calliope music rang out.

"How did you do that?" she asked, stepping back to look around.

Her expression, so quizzical that Chad could almost see question marks pouring out of her head, made him laugh. "I didn't. It's just there, like the mirror. 'Harmony in Cymbals,' Dad's favorite song."

Katie returned his affectionate smile as she brushed dust off her khaki pants and surveyed the warehouse's vast piles. "This property is no good to anyone in this condition. Do you know if the camp owner still wants to buy it?"

"She does, although we haven't talked money again."

"Maybe she'll raise her offer. I like the option of it being part of a camp now, filled with children. Especially happy children."

"*Yeah!*" cheered a young voice.

They both froze.

"That's not coming from the mirror," Chad declared, and they easily located its source behind a stack of Skee-Ball rings. His mouth twitched when Katie peered at the kid. *She sees his resemblance to Geoff, just like I did earlier.* "What are you doing here?" he asked the boy, hoping his voice sounded stern. "Where are your scavenger hunt buddies?"

The kid tugged at a clump of his hair. "I got lost," he sputtered before running out.

While Chad made sure the kid had left the building, Katie wandered off, but he found her astride her old copper-colored carousel pony behind a row of ticket booths. "Hey, it's your Morgan horse."

"That's beside the point. Didn't you notice that kid looked like Geoff?"

"I know. He even tugged at his hair the way Geoff does." Chad opened a crate, pulling out some fiberglass insulation.

"Have you talked to Geoff?"

"Not yet," he responded, shutting the crate. "Get off that horse, it's really dirty. You're kind of a mess, in fact."

Katie sniffed, dismounting with as much dignity as possible. "You mind your business," she ordered. But when she looked down at her clothes, she gave him a rueful smile. "Glad I came anyway."

"Me too. Let's head outside. I have some towels in my truck."

As they left, she said, "So how will we convince Geoff?"

"I'm not sure," he replied, "but we're going to think up something."

～⁛～

That night, Katie used her elbow to push the microwave

door shut and poured steaming popcorn into a large bowl. She munched a handful, marveling again at the chance encounter with Geoff that afternoon.

After she and Chad had arrived home from Carnival King, they'd talked in the road, and Geoff's car came screeching around the corner. Instead of turning into his driveway, he pulled up alongside them. "Don't you two know better than to play in the streets?" he joked, breaking the ice. They'd made plans to discuss L.U.C.K. at Katie's that night.

Where's Chad? He promised to be here by now. Despite the brand-new thaw between them, she'd rather not face Geoff alone. The doorbell chimed. Grabbing the popcorn, she ran to answer it.

They'd both arrived simultaneously. Chad studied his fingernails. Geoff flipped his phone shut and put it into his suit pocket.

"C'mon in," she said, setting her bowl on the coffee table in the living room, where Geoff took a seat on the large yellow sofa, and Chad plopped onto one of the matching chairs. "I'll be right back with sodas."

By the time she returned, Chad had filled Geoff in on Donna's call and Katie's agreement with him about selling the L.U.C.K. property to Camp Inch.

Geoff sipped from the can she handed him. "I'm not

convinced," he said. "We can do better than Donna's offer. That property is valuable. I talked to the condos people again. Their offer's still good, but they told me weeks ago they'll need an answer by..." He checked a note in his day planner. "By August sixth. So, I won't sell any other way than at market value."

"Well," said Katie carefully, from the ottoman between them, "that's where we left off last time. Can we find something that makes all three of us happy?"

"Four, if you include Pop," said Chad.

"Pop's not here to agree or disagree." When Chad raised an eyebrow at his sister, Geoff added, "What?"

"Some pretty odd stuff happened at the warehouse." Chad brushed popcorn kernels off his lap as he described the carousel music and laughter, the children in the mirror, and their father's strong presence. "Then this kid showed up out of nowhere. He wasn't an apparition, though, he was real, and he looked exactly like you when you were his age."

Geoff tugged at his spiky hair, running his fingers through it afterward to restore the stylish cut. He remained silent.

Katie moved next to him on the couch. "When I saw that kid, I realized how much I miss the way the three of us used to be." She put her hand over his. "I'm sorry we had that fight."

"I'm sorry as well," said Geoff. "You too, buddy," he said to Chad. "I said a bunch of stuff I shouldn't have."

"That goes for me too," Chad agreed.

Geoff cleared this throat. "I never told either of you, but the last time we were there together…" He seemed to be searching for words. "During the argument, I had every intention of selling to the condos people whether you wanted to or not. I knew that as executor, I could do it legally. And besides, it would be a lot of money for all of us. Anyway, right when I was about to let you know I was going ahead with my plan, the strangest thing happened. Something… I mean someone… I don't know what it was, but it felt like someone was standing behind me with a hand on my shoulder. And I heard this soft whisper, 'Don't.'"

Chad stopped tossing a small couch pillow. He let out a long whistle.

"So, I didn't."

Katie hugged her knees to her chest. "Something's reaching out to all of us."

"Maybe," said Geoff. "I'm not sure about selling to Camp Inch, and I definitely will not sell below market value, but I won't do anything without all of us agreeing. How's that?"

"Thanks, bro." said Katie, and Chad added, "I'll talk to Donna."

Geoff got up to go, giving a hug and accepting an invitation to dinner that weekend. "Can Miranda and I bring anything?"

"No thanks, I'm set," she replied. "Chad, your girlfriend's still coming, right? I can't wait to meet her."

"Yep," he said. "I wouldn't want her to miss one of your famous dinner parties."

The men took off, and Katie whistled a few bars of "Harmony in Cymbals" as she closed the front door.

Chapter Eighteen

JULY 2

Geoff spent a restless night struggling for an explanation of Katie's remark that "something's reaching out to all of us." *What is it?*

The next morning, he cancelled his appointments and drove to Leroy Usher, Carnival King. Relishing the thought of how much the property's market value had increased during the last few months, he lowered the car's top and lifted his face to the fresh summer sky. With an eye out for the family's totem pole landmark, he circled onto White Falls Highway, pulled over, and examined its glossy surface. *Other than a recent paint job, it looks like it always did.*

A few minutes later, he unlocked L.U.C.K.'s wooden doors and stepped into the quiet gray foyer. Sunlight illuminated a path through the dusty crates. His footsteps made the only sound. The silence was eerie after Chad's and Katie's description of laughter and music.

With little room to maneuver, Geoff located the funhouse mirror they said had seemed to offer a glimpse into the past. Rubbing its dusty surface with a handkerchief, he peered in, then backed away, surprised by the sudden quickening of his heart. When his pants leg caught on a crate's rough edge, he inspected it for damage, glad to find none.

Rather than confront the mirror again right away, he surveyed the room, crammed with useless junk. He envisioned it as a shopping mall split into multiple floors and doodled in his day planner, listing some notes for a revenue stream from advertisers. He brightened at an idea to cover the orange paint outside in murals aimed at residents of condos sprinkled around the property.

Finally, out of distractions, he gathered his nerve and turned back to the mirror where his body stretched up like a beanpole in the curved Plexiglas. When he shifted right, it blew out like a balloon. He counted thirty seconds. Nothing changed.

That's it? He tried again, but when the mirror displayed only his stretched-out self, he tugged at his hair, sighing in frustration.

What a waste of time. *Katie and Chad might have wanted to see that spooky stuff more than they truly saw it*, he reasoned, hurrying outside and locking up. *Maybe that's what happened here to me last winter too.*

Driving off, he placed a call to the condo's rep, leaving a message suggesting they consider upping their price to insure a winning offer.

─ ⁊ ─

After breakfast the next morning, Darby caught up with the boys on Branch Hall's porch. Justin told them about his visit to L.U.C.K., elevating her spirits with news of Chad's and Katie's reconciliation. But when Naz unwrapped the paperweight, her face fell.

"It hasn't changed at all," she exclaimed.

"Are you sure?" asked Justin.

Naz sighed. "You see the mark I made at halfway? The orange line has not moved past it."

They put their heads together for a closer look.

Naz handed the paperweight to Darby. "You must keep it," he said, his voice quivering. "Perhaps I did something to break it."

She shook it, but the orange line held still, and she gave it back. "No, you're doing fine."

"Maybe something went wrong," said Justin.

Darby looked away, running through likely explanations. "Naz and I didn't make it there, but you went. That should have been enough. Shouldn't it?" She waited for some reassuring calliope music to answer, but none came.

"I bet it'll move soon," said Justin. On their way inside, he reminded Darby to meet him in the afternoon for a singing lesson. "Up there." He motioned to the second floor. "It's the last door to the right."

"Okay," she said, but the prospect only increased her discontent.

A few hours later, Darby opened the Music Room door and peeked around cautiously, as if she'd entered a haunted house. One end held a small stage. An upright piano at the opposite end sat between two large windows overlooking the same grove of trees she'd seen yesterday outside the infirmary. Next to the doorway, folding metal chairs and black music stands lay stacked on rolling carts beside a drum set with a sparkly metallic blue finish.

An imposing gold harp in the corner drew Darby inside. She plucked a few of its thick strings then strummed her fingers across them, wincing at the clashing jangle. *That's what I'll sound like.* She closed her eyes, almost hearing the mocking laughter she imagined greeting her during the Talent Show. *What if I trip on the stage? What if I fall off?* Her jaw clenched. *Is it too late to tell Justin I can't rehearse today? Or ever?*

Seconds later, he arrived carrying several music books. "You made it," he said. "I wasn't sure you would."

"I wasn't either. I almost left just now."

"Look through this." He handed her one of the music books, taking the others to the piano. "I'm pretty sure you'll know one."

She flipped through the pages. "I probably do, but I don't know if I can sing without stuttering. Or even in tune." Then she chuckled. "Where did you get this? The people on the cover look so old fashioned."

"The library. It was these or opera." Justin ran his fingers up and down the keyboard, practicing scales before launching into a popular tune.

Darby leaned on the piano lid. "You're really good," she said. "I wish I was really good at something."

"Didn't you tell me you have a bunch of riding trophies?"

"I guess," she admitted.

"That's pretty cool. Probably takes a lot of practice... like working on a song?" He grinned.

Unsmiling, Darby folded her arms across her chest.

"I'll teach you this one. The first note is a D. Like in Darby," he joked.

Her reply this time was a scowl.

During the next half hour, he played the song at least a dozen times while she did the best she could to follow along.

"Sing louder," he urged over and over. "I can't hear you."

"You're p-p-playing too loud," she finally complained. "Isn't it g-g-good enough that I learned most of the words already?"

"Um, not really," he began, but Darby stopped him, pointing to a name in the music book. "Who's this? Lib... lib... – How do you say that again?"

"Libb-er-ah-chee. Liberace. He was a famous singer," Justin

replied, finding a black and white photo in another songbook.

At the sight of the entertainer's exaggerated pompadour hairstyle, Darby's irritated expression dissolved into a smile. Temporarily.

"Let's try it one more time, then I have to go," he said.

She sighed and gripped the music, her neck muscles tightening as they worked through the song. "How was th-th-that?"

Justin hesitated; doubt written all over his face. "It was... better. And the Talent Show is still more than a month away." Leaving Darby with the books, he ran off to a swim session.

Sitting alone at the piano, she stared at the keys for at least five minutes before pressing the D key. She whispered the lyrics, elongating them into something resembling a musical note. She raised her voice, stopping abruptly at a scratching sound at the door. *Was that a knock?*

After silence followed, she labored through the song again, keeping her voice as loud as she could, but freezing at an unmistakable noise in the hallway. She ran to the door and opened it in time to see Jessica and June running down the landing to the stairs, laughing merrily.

Darby slammed the door shut, slumping stock still against it. Mortification turned her face deep red. *All things are NOT possible.* Tears rolled down her cheeks. *I'll never be able to do this.*

Chapter Nineteen

With her heart no longer pounding and her face returning to its normal color, Darby gathered up the music books. She'd already discarded her original idea to toss them out so Justin could never borrow them again. But in case the twins had snuck back, she left via the stage's back door, which led through a bathroom to another exit into the hall.

A notice on the library's floor-to-ceiling shelves read PLEASE RETURN WHAT YOU BORROW IN THE SAME PLACE. Staring up at all the books, she found the Music section and slid hers in there. Underneath, an oversized *Moths and Butterflies* picture book near the Nature label caught her eye. Its color photographs brought a smile to her face. *This is perfect for tonight.*

Back at Six South, where most of her cabin mates were lounging on their bunks, she almost tripped over June and Jessica on the floor. When they halted their game of jacks and whispered to each other, she backed out the door, holding her book tightly.

"Darby," called Monica, "What's that?"

With a wary glance at the twins, Darby returned and sat

beside her friend on Lindsay's bunk. "It's got a picture of the Moraga moth I was telling you about this morning."

"Oooh, it's beautiful." Lindsay took the book and read the caption below a vivid photo of the spectacular creature. "The Moraga moth is indig... indig... how's that pronounced?"

"Indigenous." Darby smiled at how sometimes the hardest words came so easily.

"Okay. The Moraga moth is indigenous to the Northern Midwestern states. Its wingspan ranges from three to six inches, and its palette of colors includes blue, green, violet, red, and yellow. Never seen in daylight, this moth is seldom spotted even after dark, though it is attracted to sources of light."

"Moths!" gasped June, her disdain thicker than Darby's book.

"Yeah," chimed in Jessica, "don't they eat holes in your sweaters?"

Darby flushed. "It's n-n-not a j-j-joke," she attempted. "I-I-I'm sure I s-s-saw one last year."

The twins traded a triumphant glance.

Monica tugged Darby's sleeve. "Listen," she whispered, leaning her head in. "Let them think what they want."

"I'm s-s-sick of them," Darby lamented, hyperventilating with frustration.

Lindsay drew close. "It's not only you. They're that way

with everyone. Remember after square dancing when they got called into Donna's office for making fun of Cowboy Bob?"

Darby nodded.

"My mom told me that the best thing to do when someone upsets me is ignore them," said Monica. "Nothing works better."

"Really?" said Darby, fighting tears.

"What are you whispering about?" called Jessica.

"Killer bugs?" snickered June.

Uncertain, Darby bit her lip. This time, instead of responding, she turned a few pages in the book, pointing to other photos with her pals. "Wow, look at that!"

"What*ever*," yawned Jessica, turning away.

Monica and Lindsay gave Darby a thumbs up, and she returned the gesture with a conspiratorial smile.

That evening, Darby stuck out her marshmallow over a roaring campfire that tossed burnt-orange light around the Wild Strawberries' circle of faces. After the outsides had turned golden, she slurped in its oozing sweetness and gazed up. The sky still showed light blue on the horizon, but a few stars sparkled directly above. Darkness dimmed the lacquered tables' bright colors.

"Hurry and finish," called Counselor Rochelle. "We'll be starting sky games in a minute."

"We'll look for a Moraga moth, too, won't we?" asked Darby, not for the first time that day.

"Sure, we can try. But they're super rare."

While the Wild Strawberries scanned the sky to identify Orion and other constellations, Darby felt for the butterfly net she'd secured to her belt. She scoured the cookout area's ring of tall lights, all surrounded by buzzing insects. Last year, when she spotted a Moraga moth in this same area, its iridescent reds, greens, violets, yellows, and blues had dazzled her to dizziness. *Kind of like when we flew on Mr. Usher's trolley the first time.*

After Rochelle's sky games, she directed the girls to a table laid with supplies for a lightning bug search. Counselor Sally handed out flashlights and mason jars. "They can't see blue light," she said, tearing off pieces of colored plastic wrap, "so cover your flashlight with this and you won't scare them off."

With everyone equipped, the girls started toward the trees, but Darby wrinkled her nose in distaste. *Fireflies don't belong in jars.*

Chattering voices echoed in the crisp night air, while spooky blue beams darted around the trees. "I got one!" yelled Austine. "I mean, I think I do," she added.

Darby winced as her bunkmate slammed the top down on the jar.

"Look, some of the glow stuff's on your sleeve," observed

Maria.

"I've got ten already!" said June, her container flickering with frenzied pin-size amber lights.

To Darby, the bugs seemed desperate to escape. "Let them go! Let them go!" she pleaded. "They can't breathe."

"Don't freak out," June retorted.

"It's okay," said Rochelle. "They can live in the jar for a while, especially since we put wet towels on the bottom for humidity. We'll free them before too long."

As the others wandered on, Jessica set a jar on the ground near Darby. "Unless, of course, someone is clumsy enough to knock over the jar, and the lid comes off," she snickered.

"And the bugs crawl out," June joined in, "and someone *happens* to step on them. Wouldn't that be terribly sad?"

"You're absolutely right. It could happen," added Jessica with a leer.

Darby's face darkened in fury. But with Monica's advice to ignore taunts still fresh, she gritted her teeth. Gathering all the restraint she could muster, she turned away.

Surprised, the twins shrugged, picked up the jar, and joined the others.

Briefly consoled by her unfamiliar achievement, Darby stood alone for a minute then snuck back to the cookout area where a few logs still smoldered in the fire pit. When she stabbed them with a long stick, an exploding shower of sparks revived the flames.

She perched on a low stump, pulled the blue wrap off her flashlight, and pointed it skyward, her butterfly net in place. *Not to capture the moth, only to hold it for a quick glimpse.*

The night was quiet and still except for a low murmur of voices and a loud screech every now and then from one of the girls.

Darby searched every source of illumination, her eyes roaming from the light poles to her flashlight to the fire pit and back again. Shivering after the fourth round, she just about gave up when the fire's flames brightened, shooting sparks high into the air.

Wait. Those aren't sparks.

Darby rose, no longer cold. She left her butterfly net on the stump and her flashlight on the ground, heading for the fire where hundreds, maybe thousands, of lightning bugs hovered over the logs. They blinked on and off like turn signals.

Soon, they formed cylinders and rose above the pit. Darby held her breath as the spiraling brightness merged into an astonishing mass that moved toward her. She backed up, stumbling a bit, but kept her balance.

"Where are you going?" she asked, not really expecting an answer.

The fireflies circled past. Her expectant eyes were glued to the glowing insects. They headed for the stump, swirling in and out of her net. Seconds later, they dissolved in the darkness. Darby exhaled, tingling in awe.

When she grabbed the butterfly net, a small slip of paper fluttered to the ground. Her heart pounding, she pointed the flashlight to read its red type.

All things *are* possible. Keep going!
L.U.

Chapter Twenty

JULY 5

Naz sat on the edge of his bed wiping sleep from his eyes after his counselor woke the Rangers well before morning bugle call to explore ideas for their booth at the camp fair.

"Men, I propose a first aid demonstration," Rich intoned to a chorus of groans.

"What about my Water Dunk plan?" asked Woody. "You know, where kids throw bean bags at a target, and if it hits hard enough, the person on the hot seat drops into a vat of water."

Despite enthusiasm buzzing around the cabin, Rich snapped, "Too complicated. And who's sitting on the hot seat?" he demanded. "Not me."

"Can we ask other counselors?" suggested Naz.

"Great idea," said Woody. "How about we all ask someone on staff to volunteer?"

Rich fiddled with his whistle. "All right," he said to cheers from the Rangers.

At lunch that afternoon, Naz considered candidates. *Maybe Justin's counselor. Or Cowboy Bob. Or the camp director!* he thought, as Donna stopped at the Rangers' table and beamed in approval when some of the boys described their camp fair plans.

He stood up. "May I ask a question of you?"

"Certainly, dear, what is it?"

"Will you..." he paused. "Will you..." he repeated, unable to remember the English words Woody used earlier. Stares from everyone at the table silenced his tongue. Finally, he blurted it out in French. "*Seriez-vous offrir a participer a notre jeu?*"

Rich, his voice as dark as his face, slammed his hand on the table. "English."

Overwhelmed, Naz ran out Branch Hall's door and curled himself up in a chair on the back porch. He covered his eyes, waiting for a whistle screech to summon him back.

Instead, someone said, "Naz, dear."

When he turned his head, he found Donna pulling up a chair next to him.

"I was not able to think of the correct words," he said, his expression matching his miserable tone. "I am sorry."

"No," she said, "I should apologize to you. I told Rich to make sure you spoke English as your mother requested so you'd continue to learn, with Woody's help. I didn't realize he would take it so literally, and now he understands."

Naz smiled, straightening up in the chair.

"Meanwhile," she continued, handing him a pocket-size volume whose cover read *English/French Vocabulary and*

Pronunciation, "I studied French before my trip to Paris last fall, and I think this might be as helpful to you as it was to me."

"Thank you," said Naz, as surprised as he was relieved.

"*De rien*," she responded, adding a compliment, also in French. "You have been working very hard, and your parents will be proud. Now, let's go back inside so you can finish lunch and share the news that I've volunteered to be your representative for the dunking booth."

Chapter Twenty-One

JULY 15

Darby's mind wandered as the Wild Strawberries watched a rock-climbing instruction video in Branch Hall, her concern rising at a notion that would not go away. *Two weeks since Mr. Usher invited us to the warehouse. Longer than ever before. Something must have gone wrong after Justin went by himself.*

Since then, she'd talked to the boys daily, but every check-in brought no news and no movement in the orange line. Still, she clung to Mr. Usher's encouragement to "Keep going." *Maybe tomorrow.*

~ॐ~

JULY 22

Another week passed. Still nothing. During arts and crafts, while Justin worked on his bird feeder, he added up the days left until August sixth, as if he hadn't already counted squares on the bathroom calendar grid that morning. *Just over two weeks. That can't be right.*

Franklin interrupted Justin's attempt at a recount when he asked the Charging Buffaloes to think about ideas for the Talent Show.

"We can tell jokes," suggested Eugene.

"We can?" Justin stopped threading wire around his feeder's

twigs. "I don't know any good ones. Besides," he began, but Eugene interrupted, offering to get his mom to mail his joke book.

Before Justin could talk Eugene out of it, the other boys agreed, and Franklin told everyone to pair up. "We still have plenty of time until the Talent Show," he said, "so let's see what we come up with."

On the way back to the cabin, as Justin accepted Eugene's invitation to partner, his empathy rose for Darby's reluctance to perform. "It's hard to make people laugh," he groused.

"I already know some jokes," Eugene assured him, "so don't worry. It'll work great."

Behind them, Kenny hooted. "Perfect, the swimming pool cheater and the food freak."

Justin froze in his tracks. He didn't care what names Kenny directed his way, but taunts at Eugene, the first buddy his age that he'd had in a long time, enraged him. "You better take that back."

Kenny blocked their way. "Who's going to make me?" he said with a smirk.

Eugene held his breath, looking from one to the other.

Justin fixed a stare on Kenny, his expression forcing the burly kid to back up. "Do you want to find out?"

"Okay, all right, I take it back," conceded Kenny. "If you

can't take a joke, maybe you can't tell one either."

As he hurried away, Eugene laughed, and Justin cooled off. "I don't think he meant that to be as stupid as it was."

"Exactly." Eugene stuck out his hands, reminding Justin of a character on *Saturday Night Live*. "Listen to this one. Two loaves of bread wanted to get married, so they eloafed."

"Uh," said Justin, wincing, "Let's keep trying."

After lunch, Naz grabbed a banana and settled on Branch Hall's porch.

Dearest Naz,

Your summer adventures sound absolutely marvelous, particularly your square dancing. I am also delighted you wrote to Papá, as is he.

With my busy rehearsal and teaching schedule, I have not had much time to make many new friends, but Justin's mother and I have met for lunch a number of times. She enjoys hearing about opera, and I enjoy our conversations. When you and Justin return from camp, we agreed we'll make plans for you boys to get together.

Naz bent forward, trying to read the beginning of the next

sentence, but it had been scratched out. When he held up Mamá's peach-colored stationery to the sun, it seemed like she'd written, "Life is short, so…" *What does that mean?* Unsure, he returned to the words that followed, and his face lit up.

I have given much thought to your proposal that Papá, you, and I live together here for part of the year and at home the rest. I do not know how it could work or whether it would even be possible, but I hope you will be pleased to know that we are considering our options.

Will you continue your wonderful correspondence when you have time? I miss you buckets-full!

With love from Mamá

Having already vowed to speak only English until camp ends, Naz pulled out Donna's book to make sure "considering our options" translated to the meaning he supposed. He looked up considering and pronounced its definitions one syllable at a time. "Dis-cuss. Ex-plore. In-ves-ti-gate."

After repeating them a few times, he concluded with an American phrase he'd discovered last week. "Way to go." Then he headed back into the dining room for the daily rendezvous, spotting Justin at the nearly empty Charging Buffaloes table. "My Mamá talked with your Mamá," said Naz, showing him her letter, "and she said we can hang out together when we return from camp."

"Yeah, my mom told me too," Justin replied, waving his own letter. "It'll be fun."

Eugene returned from dropping off his tray. "I found another joke for our routine. Can I test it on you two?"

Justin polished off his nectarine. "Sure, go ahead."

"Knock, knock," said Eugene.

"Who's there?"

"Cows go."

"Cows go who?"

"No, cows go MOO!" finished Eugene.

"I don't understand," said Naz, while Justin sighed.

"What?" Eugene collapsed onto a bench. "It's funny, isn't it?"

"Well, it's no worse than the rest," Justin replied. "They don't have to be great, you know. None of the other guys are going to be that hilarious."

Seemingly comforted, Eugene pulled out a pen.

When Darby knocked on the window, Naz and Justin slipped outside, leaving Eugene scribbling in his notebook.

"Anything?"

The boys shook their heads.

"Me neither," she said, dropping onto the steps with her head on her knees.

Naz kicked at the balustrade.

Justin sat beside her. Laughter from campers on the Great Lawn sounded far away. "I think I know why we haven't heard from Mr. Usher and why the orange line hasn't moved," he began. "I didn't want to say this before 'cause I didn't want you to feel bad about not being able to come last time. But I'm not sure that everything worked right since you guys weren't there."

"I knew it," lamented Darby, "because Mr. Usher already said that every time all three of us are there, it affects 'matters yet to come.' Remember?"

"Matters yet to come," echoed Naz. "Will they not happen now?"

"He didn't exactly say that," Darby replied, her expression apprehensive. "But you see what I mean?"

Justin's eyes met hers in dismay. "Today's July twenty-second. We only have until August sixth. Sixteen days to go."

"He won't be able to reunite with his wife if we don't do something." She shook her head. "But what?"

"Here is an idea," said Naz, who interrupted himself periodically to consult his dictionary. "Mr. Usher advised us to bring what we learned at L.U.C.K. into our lives, so I did that when I wrote Papá about my idea for him to live with Mamá and me. And the line moved. Now I have decided to speak only English, because I am not sure I can. Perhaps it will help."

Justin nodded. "I told you about my dad and hung out with my cabin mates, stuff I didn't want to do. The line moved then too."

They looked at Darby. She picked at a strand of grass and shredded it into pieces. "Um... he told me to keep going," she offered.

Around the corner, a mild breeze rustled some wind chimes.

"Was that our magic music?" asked Naz, his eyes dancing.

"All things are possible," said Justin.

"Maybe," said Darby, her voice barely audible. "Maybe not."

Chapter Twenty-Two

JULY 28

Katie met Chad in his driveway, and they drove together to the meeting he'd arranged with Donna. His truck rumbled onto White Falls Highway, where afternoon sunlight enveloped the trees in a golden haze. Donna greeted them in the parking lot, guiding them to her office past crowds of campers lounging on the lawn and Branch Hall's porch. "It's Free Time Hour," she explained over playful shouts and animated conversations. They settled on the ladder-back armchairs in front of her desk.

"Well?" she said.

Katie took the lead. "We're all in agreement about selling the property."

"Great," said Donna. "Right?"

"Yes and no," Chad responded. "Geoff has a bid from a real estate developer that's one third higher than yours, and they need an answer at the end of next week. So, we're kind of stuck again."

"I see." Donna slumped in her chair and gazed through the window, then turned back, her posture straightening. "Well, if it's just about finding additional monies, I can look into that."

Katie exchanged a glance with her brother at a note of uneasiness that seemed to color Donna's words.

"Meanwhile," she continued, "let me take you on a camp tour."

Chad accepted her offer of a snack, while Katie asked for the restroom.

"Use the one upstairs," said Donna, heading to the kitchen, "If you miss the hallway door, go in through the Music Room. It'll be empty at this time of day."

Under Justin's orders, Darby had grudgingly agreed to spend part of her Free Time Hours practicing. Yesterday they'd worked together, but today the Charging Buffaloes had journeyed to Barton Flats.

Alone in the Music Room with the songbook propped open, Darby slumped over the piano and pounded the D key. To avoid falling asleep from boredom, she looked around, hoping to spot something more entertaining than musical instruments. *Wait!* She jerked fully upright. *Justin's gone. There's no reason I couldn't leave right now. He'll never know.*

After checking to be sure of an empty hallway, she grabbed the music book and skipped toward the stairway. Inside the Game Room, a calendar with an array of horse photos caught her attention. She looked closer. Someone had put an X on all the squares in July up through yesterday.

Darby focused on today's date: July 28, 1999. *Three days till*

August. She shuddered. *Still nothing from Mr. Usher. Still no change in the orange line.*

The songbook slipped to the floor with a thud. When she stooped to pick it up, Mr. Usher's words about the orange color floated through her head, as if she'd heard them yesterday. *It grows the most if you help yourself by doing something you don't want to do.* Her stomach turned over. *Or something you don't think you can.*

Justin and Naz are doing their parts. But I still haven't contributed. Darby drifted into the hallway. *It worked for them. Will it work for me?* She looked toward the stairway and the Great Lawn outside. They seemed so inviting. Then she held up the music book. *Intrepid means determined. I have to keep trying, even though I don't want to.* Within seconds she was back at the piano.

As she worked on her song, the door from the back of the stage opened, and a woman peered in. "Oh, sorry," she said. "I didn't mean to interrupt."

Startled, Darby spun around on the piano stool, which spilled her onto the floor.

The tall, slim brunette, her hair tied in a braid intertwined with a white ribbon, rushed over and helped her to her feet. "Are you all right?" she asked. A flash of astonishment replaced her concern.

"Yeah," replied Darby, reddening under the woman's burning stare.

After an awkward pause, the woman said, "Sorry. You remind me of... someone else."

Darby found her face familiar, too.

"My name is Katie. My brothers and I own the land next door, and I'm on a tour of your camp."

It's Katie Usher! she realized, overjoyed at the idea that she might be as pretty when she grew up. "I-I-I'm Darby."

"Nice to meet you." Katie bent toward the music book. "Can you play that song?"

"No." Darby sighed. "I can't even sing it, and I'm supposed to l-l-learn it for the T-T-Talent Show." Something in Katie's sympathetic smile prompted her to confide, "When I think about getting up in front of people, my throat closes up. Especially when people l-l-laugh at me." Her face colored again.

"Wow, you're bringing back some of *my* childhood memories."

Darby noticed that the woman's eyes seemed glossy.

"I'm glad we've met," Katie continued, "because I felt that way for a long time when I was your age, but also when I was older." She reached out to pat Darby's shoulder. "You should know that it can change."

Doubt ran across Darby's face. Advice from adults usually

started with admonishments followed by criticisms. "How?"

"I practiced a mental exercise every day for a while. And whenever I was afraid, I practiced it again."

"What was it?"

"It sounds kind of goofy." Katie gave her a lopsided grin. "I envisioned myself as a tiny bud out in the sunshine. I didn't have to do anything except feel warm light opening me up into a beautiful flower."

The roses from Katie's garden in the cul-de-sac swam through Darby's mind.

"If I started to think about making a mistake or what people might think, I went back to focusing on myself and how the sun was affecting me. I didn't believe it could work, but I was told to pretend that it would. And to trust that it would. After a while, it did. I'm a teacher now, so I get up in front of people all the time." Katie added, "Try it."

Closing her eyes, Darby pictured sunny warmth calming and encouraging her. She gasped as lightness replaced the pressure in her middle. It spread up to her head and down to her toes.

"How does it feel?"

"Kind of... kind of good." Darby's eyes opened slowly. "Thank you."

"Practice that every day if you can," said Katie. "If it worked for me, there's no reason why it won't work for you, too."

"Okay, I'll try." Darby smiled. *She's so nice. I wonder if she'll tell me anything about the warehouse sale.* "Um, are you here to t-t-talk about Camp Inch buying your property?"

Katie's forehead furrowed. "How do you know about that?"

"Well." Darby stopped. *Now what?* She fought to keep her voice from quivering. "I heard our camp director t-t-telling someone." *It's not a lie, really.* "Anyway, I hope it works out. She said your father thought it would be cool for k-k-kids to play over there." *Okay, that's a lie. Mr. Usher said that, not Donna. But maybe it will help.*

"We'll have to see." Katie headed for the door. "Wait a sec." Locating a pad of paper and pen, she tore off a sheet, scribbled down some lines, and folded it. "Here. Read this before you go to bed at night and also when you get up in the morning. It helped too."

"I will."

As Katie left, Darby returned to the piano and softly sang a few lines. To her surprise, her throat felt looser. She unfolded Katie's paper.

Every soul is worthy

Everyone's unique

Open up your spirit

Don't be afraid to speak

Your special gifts are valued

Your fears can all be faced

Live evermore to take a chance

You always will be safe.

At the bottom, it was signed, "To Darby... from K.U. (Katie)."

She swayed on the stool, almost dizzy with hope.

Down the road at Leroy Usher, Carnival King, a light in the cotton candy machine, dark for weeks, flickered on.

Katie found Chad at a table downstairs. "Sorry it took so long," she said, sliding in beside Donna as her brother scooped up the last spoonful in a bowl of green Jell-O. "I had a sweet conversation with a young girl in the Music Room." She shot him a knowing look. He raised his eyebrows, but she indicated Donna with her head, mouthing, "Later."

They spent the rest of the afternoon walking around the property, then relaxed afterward on lounge chairs at the pool while a group of boys in the water batted a beach ball.

"You've done a fine job," said Katie. "The waiting list demonstrates the demand for camper openings."

"Thank you, dear," Donna said. "We have a tremendous number of reasons for expansion."

Chad stretched out; his arms crossed behind his head. "This is the life. Maybe I'll apply for a job. The bigger the camp, the more employees you'll need."

"Don't joke," said Donna. "I will be hiring additional staff and consultants, especially during the property improvements. Your input is welcome."

Chad started to respond, halting abruptly as an olive-skinned boy climbed out of the pool in front of them, shaking water out of his ear.

Katie, who shielded her fair complexion from the sun with a large straw hat, stifled a laugh at her brother's reaction to the boy, which matched her own to Darby earlier.

"Naz," yelled a camper in the pool, hitting the beach ball with his palm. "Catch this."

It landed on Katie's lap, and the kid ran up to collect it. She held onto the ball, captivated by his eyes, which seemed even bluer than her brother's. Finally, she gave it back, and he jumped into the pool.

On the ride home, she marveled, "There are *three* of them at the camp. One that looks like each of us. And the girl told me she overheard Donna say that Dad wanted kids playing over at the warehouse."

"Is that some kind of cosmic sign that the sale should work out?" asked Chad.

"I think so," she said. "I hope so."

⁓ꝏ⁓

"It moved," Darby shrieked, holding the paperweight aloft in victory when Naz pulled it out that evening before dinner. "A lot."

"It's three quarters around now," said Justin, raising his fist. "What happened?"

Darby gave a blow-by-blow account of her encounter with Katie, then Naz shared his pool story. "By the time I figured out who they were," he said, "they were walking away."

Justin chortled. "They must be flipped out," he said, turning to Darby, "and you made the line move."

"Yep, I tried s-s-something I didn't want to do. But," she said, her insides still light, "since we still haven't heard from Mr. Usher, and August sixth is a week from Friday, we have to keep going, like he asked." She threw up her hands in pretend horror. "So, can you p-p-practice with me after we eat?"

"Sure." Justin grinned. "Sounds like Mr. Usher isn't the only one in that family who works magic."

Chapter Twenty-Three

JULY 29

As a cloudless sky predicted perfect weather, Justin and his cabin mates put finishing touches on their booth for Camp Inch's inaugural Great Fair. They hung crepe paper swirls and strung colored lights, while the counselors inflated balloons. Finally, they tacked up a "Ride Into Your Future With the Charging Buffaloes" sign lettered in black on a yellow background.

A few weeks before, Emmanuel had proposed a food booth, then Hugh suggested karate lessons. But when Justin came up with the idea of reading fortunes, everyone had agreed. Except Eugene.

"How would that work?" he'd questioned. "We're not licensed for that."

A chorus of catcalls ensued.

"It doesn't have to be real," Justin had said. "We can make stuff up and write it on strips of paper."

"Let's cover a soccer ball with foil to make a crystal ball," Kenny had said, and Harper added, "We can tie Woody's red bandana around our heads."

In the end, everyone, even Eugene, had approved, and they

were ready when the Great Fair kicked off with a string of lively songs blasting from loudspeakers.

Naz's shift at the Rangers' booth ended after what turned out to be the longest line of the day queued up to dunk Donna. Armed with a lengthy strip of prize tickets, he surveyed the red and white canopy-covered structures lining the ball field. Then he headed straight for A CANDY APPLE A DAY, his mouth watering over the choices: bright red or gooey caramel.

"Welcome to the Wild Strawberries booth," said the girl in charge. "Which flavor would you like?"

He moved his eyes back and forth. "One of each, please." Grasping the sturdy white sticks she handed over, Naz dug into the caramel. "Wild Strawberries," he said, tossing out the remains. "Is this Darby's booth?"

"Yes, you missed her though. She went to get a tattoo."

"Thanks." Naz started in on the candy apple, careful not to drop any of the crunchy red coating. He paused at Dragons Present Art by D. Vin Shee but decided against a caricature in favor of the Black-Eyed Bees' Root Beer Float Saloon. By the time he arrived at Crazy Eights' Tattoos, she had moved on.

At the end of the day, Darby met up with the boys for their regular check-in outside Justin's Ride Into the Future booth.

Anything yet from Mr. Usher? In response to her shared thought, they shook their heads. "We're running out of time." She rubbed her arm on her forehead.

"Uh-oh," said Justin, "you've smeared your Wonder Woman tattoo."

"It washes off anyway," Darby grumbled.

Naz pointed at the Charging Buffaloes' sign. "I have two tickets left. Perhaps we will find out something here."

"Guys," said Justin, "these fortunes are just stuff me and my cabin mates made up."

"Even so, we must make an attempt." Naz quoted the paperweight. "'All that we give comes back to benefit ourselves.'"

Darby shrugged, but she and Justin followed him inside, where Eugene presided behind the booth's black-draped counter, his bandana askew. Pursing his lips, he asked, "May I predict your future?"

Naz took a seat and offered his hand.

Eugene recoiled. "You're *filthy*!" He pulled a wet wipe from his back pocket and cleaned Naz's fingers. "We don't read hands anyway." Yanking the bandana back to the center of his forehead, he pressed his palms onto the foil-covered soccer ball, his eyes ablaze. "You have now entered the land of the charging buffalo," he chanted, then peered at Naz around the ball. "You know, this isn't real, right?"

"I still want my fortune," Naz insisted, so caught up in Eugene's act that Darby snickered.

"Don't worry." Eugene snapped back into character. "Your every question will be answered!"

"When shall we hear from Mr. Usher?"

"I only convey what I am shown in the Great Ball," hissed Eugene. "Stop breaking the flow."

"Sorry!" Naz squeaked.

Eugene reached underneath the counter, pulled out a slip of paper, quickly read it, and handed it to Naz. "This fortune predicts you will become very rich," he declared, his tone dramatic.

"What? I don't want to become like Rich!"

"Hush," ordered Eugene. "Fortune number two predicts that he who wears no suspenders may lose pants."

Naz turned to the others. "I don't understand."

Darby just shook her head, trying not to roll her eyes.

With an imperious glare, Eugene motioned her to take Naz's place in the chair. "Are you prepared to discover the future?" he demanded.

"Actually, yes." She threw the boys a wistful glance. "More than anything."

"Good. You have now entered the land of the charging

buffalo," Eugene chanted. "Your every question will be answered." He reached down and handed a fortune to Darby. "This predicts you will bring happiness to millions."

"Millions?" She stared at the black handwriting on the slip of lined notebook paper.

"Hey," said Justin, "That's one of mine."

"Silence!" Eugene commanded. "The messages are coming very fast today." With one palm on the foil-covered ball, and the other under the table, he kept his eyes down.

"And now," he announced, "your second and final fortune." His eyes flew open, and he lost his bandana, breaking character completely. "This doesn't seem like any of the ones we wrote," he said, handing it to Darby. "I have no idea what it means."

The moment she touched the stiff parchment, entirely different from her first fortune, and read its words, she jumped up, and held it aloft. "YEAH!" she yelled, passing it to Justin.

His mouth fell open.

Naz grabbed it. "'You will be Ushered onto wings of fancy tomorrow night!'"

"Typed," Darby added, "in red letters."

"I don't understand," said Eugene, rummaging through the remaining paper slips in the fortune box. "What's going on?"

Justin pushed Darby and Naz outside. "Eugene, you did great," he called back. "You should be an actor."

Without waiting for a reply, they took off for the cookout area, howling with laughter and banging their fists on the lacquered tables. When Darby caught her breath, she flopped onto the bench. "How did Mr. Usher make *that* happen?"

"I wish I knew," said Justin, his elation matching hers.

Naz kept bouncing up and down on his toes. "How does he do all the things he's done?"

"I doubt we'll ever know," she replied, "but it doesn't matter as long as there's still time to finish the orange circle."

The trio ambled back to the fair, where colored lights cast a warm glow over the field, crepe paper swirls hung limp with evening dampness, and loudspeakers wound down with classic tunes. After a chorus of male voices crooned lyrics about saying goodnight, Darby shared an amused look with Justin when the song she'd been practicing came on. She struck a silly pose with her hand behind her head, mouthing along.

Just then, a shooting star streaked brilliantly across the darkness.

Darby tingled, as optimistic as she'd ever been. "This might be the best summer I've ever had."

Chapter Twenty-Four

MIDNIGHT...

At L.U.C.K. the next night, Darby stood before Timeless Voyages' curtained doorways, circling from one option to another. She'd already ruled out Western Stagecoach, Mystery Island, and Journey to Mars. Twirling a lock of hair, she weighed The Chambered Nautilus against Unconventional Flight, settling on the former. But as Mr. Usher reached to pull aside a blue curtain, she stopped him. *The fortune said wings of fancy.* "Let's do Unconventional Flight instead."

He pointed Darby and the boys through its crimson opening to a wide stairway. On the landing, a pair of old movie theatre-style doorways flew open, releasing a blast of bright light and buzzing noises.

"Sounds like a bunch of displeased bees," whispered Naz.

Although Darby was tempted to run the other way, she followed Mr. Usher anyway. Inside the vast space, a collection of bees, dragonflies, ladybugs, and butterflies did indeed reside, but she relaxed as she realized that none seemed angry — or even real. Unlike their living counterparts, these were gigantic bug-shaped fiberglass carriages that stood humming, vibrating, and squeaking on an elevated horseshoe-shaped track.

The rails curved toward two arched tunnels in the far wall where picnicking families on a painted mural enjoyed a sunny afternoon. A sign rose above them with "Unconventional Flight" spelled out in rustic brown lettering.

Mr. Usher led Darby and the boys through a turnstile and up a ramp covered with synthetic grass. At the top, he pushed up an instrument panel's large metal lever. Pulleys and gears ground into motion. The carriages lurched forward, releasing a distinctive smell that reminded her of hot oil. As one car disappeared into the tunnel on the right, she saw another emerge from the left.

While the boys hooted at the oversized sunglasses on a bee and a Fedora-topped dragonfly, Darby focused on the butterflies, their long black antennae curving above bulging dark eyes and their painted wings aloft.

But then, a new creature glided out of the tunnel, much larger and more elegant than the other carriages. Feathery antennae, bisected by a dark filament, contrasted with those on the butterflies. Wings rose larger in front and smaller toward the rear. It stopped at Darby's feet, as if waiting for her to board.

"This one's not like the others," said Darby, hypnotized as the wings glowed blue, then green, violet, red, and yellow. She flashed a grin of recognition at Mr. Usher. "It's a Moraga moth!"

He nodded.

Darby settled next to Justin into its molded front seats, and Mr. Usher took a rear seat beside Naz. With a clank, the safety bars pulled into place. The carriage sailed forward until the tunnel enveloped them in pitch-black darkness. They sped up slightly as the track sloped upward, pressing her against the back of the seat.

Uh oh. Anticipating a sharp roller coaster-style drop, she grabbed her safety bar, holding on so tight that she barely noticed Mr. Usher's watch ticking behind her. The carriage began to vibrate, illuminating the Moraga moth's wings with changing colors. A cool wind blew, cut off, and blew again, like a rotating room fan.

Darby shivered with anticipation. Her excitement built as the Moraga moth thundered to life. Its fiberglass wings shattered like glass then inflated with translucent waves of color that shimmered like a kaleidoscope. She caught a look at Justin's face. "You're green. Now you're blue."

"You are too," he countered, his expression as expectant as hers.

The creature's black head moved side to side, the antennae reminding Darby of a symphony conductor holding two batons. Its stout body grew warm below her. The wings whooshed like wind through a tunnel, folding in and out to carry them up.

When they reached the peak, she covered her mouth, unable to decide whether to laugh or scream.

Instead of plunging down, the Moraga moth made a long, loud hiss. It sprang off the track, and swooped up toward tiny star-like lights, sending currents of air splashing into Darby's face and through her hair. Dazzling colors energized her body with lightness running up and down, the way she'd felt when Katie had described a flower bud opening up to the sun's warmth.

The moth nimbly looped down, revealing a birds-eye view of an immense metropolis spread out as far as Darby could see. Jewel-colored lights circled a large lake. Skyscrapers rose to dizzying heights. She reached toward the tall towers in a futile attempt to touch them, screeching in awe at the cityscape. When they flew lower, she spotted some landmarks. "It's Chicago. I live near here!"

While Mr. Usher's watch sped up, a pink sun broke on the horizon. They circled a modern building, and the creature landed on a penthouse-level patio ringed with slender cypress trees. Floor-to-ceiling windows surrounded a series of sliding glass doors that overlooked the deck.

Darby grabbed Justin's arm. "My mom works in this building. I'm not allowed to b-b-be here."

"As always, we can't be seen or heard," reminded Mr. Usher, stepping down around the moth's lowered wings.

"Oh, right." Ready to explore, Darby scrambled onto the pebbled surface. At once, she stopped short and pointed to a woman engaged in conversation on a flip phone at an umbrella-topped table. "My mom!"

The woman had taken no notice of the landing, her business suit unruffled by the turbulence and scattered leaves. She finished the call, and her heels made crunching sounds on the gravel as she departed through one of the sliding glass doors.

Darby ran to a window, cupping her hands around her eyes to look inside where her mother took a seat behind a large desk.

Peering in, Naz said, "She is quite beautiful!"

"I guess," shrugged Darby.

Justin recited titles from a bookshelf near the glass. "Primary Advertising Principles. Human Behavior in the Advertising Environment. Advertising for Dummies."

Darby watched her mother sip coffee and rifle through a file folder. *Just like she does after dinner at home.*

The phone rang. "Marcia McAllister."

"Have you seen today's Banks & Sons ad?" squawked a male voice from the speaker.

"I'll find it and call you back." Pressing another button, she picked up the receiver. "Maureen, I need today's Tribune immediately," she barked before slamming it down again. Then her head fell to her chest. "What have I messed up now?"

Darby uttered a soft, "*What?* My mom *never* messes anything up."

When the newspaper arrived, her mother exclaimed at what she found. She picked up the receiver and put it back. Then, with a sharp sigh, she dialed. "I have it in front of me," she said into the speaker. "Yes, I know we discussed changing that phrase."

Darby couldn't make out the words, but the man's strident tones carried outside.

"Yes, it's definitely my fault, but I-I-I..." She caught herself. "No, it won't happen again."

Darby backed away, her heart banging against her chest. "She... she...," she said to Mr. Usher, barely able to get the words out. "She stuttered. Like me."

"Indeed she did."

Darby ran to the patio table and kicked at the pebbles. No complaint she'd ever had about her mother reached the depth of this deception. As she glared in her mom's direction, her mind raced back to a conversation with her dad. *He's right. She's not perfect.*

Mr. Usher took a seat beside her.

"Why didn't my mom ever tell me she stutters like me?" she asked, shaking with outrage. "Why does she pretend that she doesn't make mistakes?"

"Perhaps your mother judges herself too harshly to share that with you," he replied, gently lifting her chin with his hand. "Not everyone has the opportunity to learn to accept that mistakes are part of life. Everyone makes them."

Mr. Usher's words sparked a startling concept. "She's a success, right? Doesn't that mean I can be too, whether I stutter or not?"

"I think you may be more fortunate than she is," he said kindly. "You already know the answer."

"We both want the best for you," her father had said. "Sometimes that ends up different from the way we mean it to sound... she loves you very much." As his comments filtered through her mind, her anger gave way to a rush of sympathy.

Darby dashed back to the screen door. Inside, her mom frowned fixedly at the newspaper.

"M-m-mom," said Darby, her tone almost shy. "Maybe you can't hear me, but please listen anyway. *Every soul is worthy... Everyone's unique,*" she recited, her confidence rising. "*Open up your spirit... Don't be afraid to speak...*"

When she concluded the second stanza, Mr. Usher coughed, his face red as he hastily replaced a white cloth in his pocket. "I see you've met my daughter," he said.

A glimmer of recognition passed over Darby. "*You* wrote that, didn't you? You're the one who taught Katie to believe she could get through the stuff that scared her."

Absorbed in his ticking watch, he didn't reply, but Darby affirmed it to the boys with a telling glance.

Mr. Usher directed them back to the moth, which had been resting contentedly in the shade, its three pairs of legs tucked underneath.

With a last look at her mother, Darby cocked her head. *She is beautiful.* Then she rushed to join the others. The Moraga moth sprang off and returned them to Unconventional Flight, the journey absolutely living up to its name.

Back in the warehouse, Mr. Usher brought them into his office. "Please wait here," he said, granting permission when Naz asked to sit in the desk chair so he could swivel side to side.

Darby stood before the wall portrait to study it closely. The dark-skinned woman's arm remained draped around the three children. But something seemed off. "What's wrong with this picture?"

"I don't know," said Justin. "It's the same as before."

"There's something weird about the way it's empty here…" she trailed off when Mr. Usher returned.

As Naz slid the chair back, the wheels stuck, and he crawled under the desk to locate the obstruction, coming up with a gold and red coin about the size of a silver dollar.

Mr. Usher, with an affectionate smile that reminded Darby

of Katie's, placed it into the desk's drawer. "Thank you. My son Geoff gave that to me. I thought it was lost."

Turning to Darby, he opened a small blue jewelry box and offered it to her. "My dear, this evening would not be complete without acknowledging the compassion you showed your mother."

Her face lit up and her eyes shone as she pulled out a gold star-shaped pendant hung from a chain. "It's beautiful, thank you." She squinted at the engraving. *Congratulations to Katie on the attainment of her teaching credential.* "Does this mean everything worked out? I mean, will our camp be buying your property?"

"We are headed in the right direction," Mr. Usher replied, taking them outside to the trolley, "but time is still short. I ask that you continue as you have. There remains more work to be done."

Chapter Twenty-Five

JULY 31

The Wild Strawberries filled the Crafts Room with chatter as they mixed paints to finish the parrot family in Jessica's mural design, and Darby gritted her teeth when Rochelle paired her with June. She worked as far from her as possible, using a wide brush to fill in some red feathers. Even so, June knocked into her arm. Hard. Darby gasped as her brush smeared a long red gash across the canvas.

June's mouth curled with scorn. "You ruined it."

"You pushed me!" Darby cried, twisting her hands.

"Go ahead and try to blame me. You're the careless one."

"N-n-no!" Darby, wincing at Jessica's stricken face. She backed away and surveyed the damage. Her eyes filled with tears, blurring the colors into a field of wildflowers. *Flowers!*

While the others examined the mural, she took a deep breath and pictured herself as a bud blooming under the sun. A sense of lightness flowing from her head to her toes gave her an idea. "If you bring me some blue paint," she told Monica, "I'll fix the papa bird. Lindsay, will you work on the babies?"

In less than five minutes, with everyone's help, the painting looked like it did before the accident.

"The colors turned out much better with some red tones," said Jessica.

"Thanks." Darby took her brushes to the sink. Out of the corner of her eye, she noticed June whispering to her sister. Instead of laughing, though, Jessica shrugged and walked out with a few other girls.

When Darby finished, she headed downstairs. Behind her, June hissed, "Lucky break." Darby started to respond. Then, instead, she caught up with Monica, Lindsay, and Austine on the way back to Six South and joined them in a giddy chorus of "John Jacob Jingle Heimer Smith."

─∾─

AUGUST 1

At Katie's urging, Geoff had agreed to check out Camp Inch. That evening he came for movie night with his wife, Miranda, whose tailored pants suit matched the sleekness of their Porsche.

"I shouldn't have worn suede," muttered Miranda, declining Donna's offer to show them around. "You two go. I'll find Katie and Chad inside."

"This is a fine place," said Geoff after the quick tour.

"Thank you, dear," Donna replied. "Your father and I frequently discussed combining the properties. I know he'd have approved. In fact, he talked as if it were his fondest wish."

His fondest wish? Geoff scoffed to himself, saying only, "Are we on track to sign on the dotted line this coming week?"

Donna hesitated. "Things are rolling along... slowly."

"Is there a problem?"

"Well, slowly, but surely." Donna checked her watch, adding brightly, "Let's go to our seats," but not before he caught a troubled expression contradicting her tone.

Darby and the Wild Strawberries headed into Branch Hall, finding its dining tables stacked along the walls. They reserved seats on two rows of the benches that faced a large movie screen. A popcorn machine drew most of her cabin mates upstairs, but Darby returned to the porch in search of Justin. Instead, she ran into Katie.

"Hey! How's the rehearsing?"

Darby flushed. "Better. A little. I've been practicing what you told me."

"That's great. My father suggested it not only for me," said Katie, "but also to pass on to others."

Without thinking, Darby exclaimed, "He was really proud when he heard me reciting your poem."

"What?" Katie's sharpness silenced everyone around them.

Almost paralyzed, Darby stuttered, "I-I-I..." which only heightened her distress. She fiddled with her necklace.

Katie seemed stunned as she spotted the gold pendant.

Darby tucked the necklace inside her shirt. She swallowed hard. Lightness, more familiar now thanks to her diligent practicing, ran up and down inside her. She met Katie's stare. "I guess I was t-t-talking about someone else," she said, fibbing easily under the circumstances.

The aroma of popping kernels drifted out the window, providing a plausible excuse to escape. "Would you like some popcorn?"

"No, thanks," answered Katie. Her voice sounded oddly high pitched. "I'll stay out here for now."

Darby sped away, buffeted equally by mortification and relief.

~⁂~

At intermission, Justin rushed upstairs for popcorn and ran into Chad.

"Hi there, remember me?"

"Uh, yes." Justin ducked his head. "I guess you remember me."

"You ran pretty fast last time we met." Chad grinned. "But I sure do."

Justin offered him a share of his popcorn. "What are you doing here?" he asked politely.

"Your camp director invited my family. We're working out

a deal so she can buy our land next door."

Justin hoped his casual tone disguised a mounting excitement. "Then it becomes part of Camp Inch?"

"I hope so. At this point, the financing decision's up to my brother."

Is that a good sign or not? Justin attempted to keep the conversation going. "Would you get to work here?"

Chad laughed. "I have thought of that." He scanned the bustling hall where some kids played popcorn "catch" and others belted out a camp song. "It might be fun."

More than fun, Justin mused, wondering if he could get Chad to hear his thoughts. *No chance.*

At the end of intermission, he scurried back to his seat, paying more attention to the prospect of locating his pals than to the film. But when he tried sending them a thought, all he heard back was a startled, "Huh?" from Darby. After the movie ended, he caught her near the exit, and they pushed through the noisy crowd to find Naz fast asleep under a column of stacked tables.

"Wake up!" Justin shook Naz's shoulder.

"I'm not asleep," he yawned, stretching his arms.

"Then what happened at the end?" Justin asked, plainly skeptical.

Naz grinned. "They all lived happily ever after."

"Okay, okay," he laughed.

"What were you trying to tell me during the show?" asked Darby. "It sounded all garbled by people in the movie."

"To meet me so I could let you know what I found out about Mr. Usher's older son..." he began, but the sound got lost in the din. "Come on, we need to talk in private." He motioned them upstairs, and they snuck into the Music Room unnoticed.

Donna invited everyone to join her for coffee, but Miranda insisted, "We have an early appointment," despite Geoff's questioning look.

"All right," he said, "let me make a pit stop before the drive."

On the way upstairs to the men's room, a framed portrait on the wall slowed him down. Something about the elderly gentleman's twinkling blue eyes and thick, wavy hair reminded him of his father.

"How do we convince Geoff that's what Mr. Usher wants," said a child's voice from inside a room.

He stepped closer. *I must have heard that wrong.*

"I kind of messed up earlier," the voice continued. "I told Katie I saw her father the other night. And she saw the pendant he gave me."

Geoff's mouth went dry. He pushed on the door, coming

face to face with two boys and a girl. *That's uncanny*, he thought, their resemblance to his siblings and himself even more startling than the way Katie and Chad described it. *Most importantly*, he realized with a jolt, *how can they have seen my father?*

The kids exchanged horrified looks.

"He heard us," whispered the younger boy.

When Geoff tried to speak, nothing came out.

"We were, um, just leaving," said the older one. He grabbed the others and dragged them out the door.

"Wait." The girl wrestled free and faced Geoff, her eyes blazing into his. "I have to tell you something."

Geoff leaned forward to peer into her face, so like his sister's. She remained stock still, but her trembling hands betrayed her.

"Your father told us he wants his property filled with happy children," she said in a shaking voice, "L-l-like kids from Camp Inch." Her tone strengthening, she added, "And he can't rest until that happens."

Before Geoff could say a word, she whirled around, dragged the boys' behind her, and disappeared out the door.

Geoff staggered to the bathroom. He splashed cold water on his white face, staring into the mirror. When something moved beside him, he started then sighed sheepishly at the sight of his shadow. Eventually he made his way outside.

"Are you all right?" Miranda asked, failing to hide her impatience.

"Yeah." He straightened his tie and tossed her the car keys. "But would you mind driving home?"

~⁂~

Darby and the boys kept running until they reached the Great Lawn.

"I can't believe you said that." Justin struggled to catch his breath.

"I don't believe it either," said Darby. "See?" She held up her palms, still trembling. "When I told Katie what Mr. Usher said, that was by accident. But this time I did it on purpose. I brought back what I learned, just like Mr. Usher asked. I hope it makes a difference – to all of us."

"I bet it will," said Justin. "'All That We Give Comes Back to Benefit Ourselves.'"

"Did you see Geoff's face?" Darby only briefly stifled a giggle.

They ran off, laughter sprinkled with calliope music trailing behind them.

~⁂~

In the office, Donna and Chad reviewed the movie's highlights, while Katie stared out the window.

"No matter how many times I see this film, I love it all over again when they reunite at the end," Donna said.

"Yep, kind of like the way you brought us back together," Chad agreed, nudging Katie.

"What? Oh, yes, thank you for that." She nodded somewhat vaguely, still preoccupied with Darby's words about their father. *And my pendant.*

"Well, not only for that," said Chad, "but also for incorporating Dad's property into Camp Inch the way he wanted."

Donna's smile faded. "I'm so sorry," she began quietly. "We may be in trouble."

Uh-oh, thought Katie, now fully attentive. "What do you mean?"

"I got word today that I can't get another loan. I thought I could, and I was going to wait for your deadline, hoping that some miracle might come to pass, but I realize now you should know where things stand."

"Oh boy," sighed Chad, exchanging a look of dismay with his sister. "Geoff won't agree to sell for anything less, especially since the condos people are talking about raising their offer. And their deadline is just five days away."

Katie rose. "I have an idea, but I need to check it out," she said. "Don't give up hope, guys. There's got to be a way."

Chapter Twenty-Six

AUGUST 2

The next morning, Geoff's car idled at a stop sign. He ran a comb through his hair, unable to get his mind off last night at Camp Inch.

It's not imagination anymore. That kid said she talked to Dad.

He revved the engine, but instead of turning toward his office, he went the opposite way and drove off to Leroy Usher, Carnival King. During the trip, he checked his voicemail, listening with pleasure to a message from the condo's rep confirming a sizable increase in their offer for the property.

Fantastic, since the camp deal seems headed south. He'd never shared Katie's and Chad's confidence that Donna could meet the market price. *Now we can get top value.*

Soon, the orange building loomed before him, its green L.U.C.K. letters gleaming. An uneasy sensation in his stomach delayed him from exiting the car for a few minutes. But once he got inside the warehouse, Geoff noted that nothing had changed since his visit a month ago. *Except more dust.*

He located the key for his father's office, as spotless as the warehouse was grubby. Pocketing his phone, he shivered with the same unease he'd felt in the car. *If someone's here, I might as well find out.* "Hello!" he called, stiffening at the possibility of a response. "Hello?"

Silence.

Geoff sat behind the desk, surveying the old-fashioned office machinery. When he punched a few buttons on the adding machine, they stuck.

Why didn't we toss this stuff when Dad died?

Spinning the dial on the rotary telephone, he recollected fruitless attempts to persuade his father to modernize. Leroy Usher loved his red phone and wouldn't hear of getting a computer or even an electric typewriter. "This Smith Corona is good enough for me," he would boom. "It's all I need."

Geoff searched the drawer for paper, rolled a sheet into the antique machine, and typed a few words, blinking with amazement that the red ribbon still worked.

Geoffrey Usher, Attorney at Law

A hunt through the drawer yielded other years-old office relics as well as his law school honors award. He held the gold and red coin, about the size of a silver dollar, in his palm. *I gave this to Dad at graduation in thanks for financial support. Also for encouragement even more generously bestowed.* The unease returned. His eyes fell on the family portrait. *Really, there was nothing Dad wouldn't do for us.*

The girl's comment last night popped into his head. "Your father told us he wants his property filled with happy children. Like kids from Camp Inch."

Leaning back in the swivel chair, Geoff wrestled with his strategy. Even the camp director confirmed Dad's desire to combine the properties. *"His fondest wish."* The condos plan and its financial bonanza inexplicably diminished in appeal. But he deliberated glumly, the likely alternative is selling for more than one-third off the price.

No, never. He crossed his arms behind his head. *Not going to happen. It's common sense to accept the higher offer.* Geoff returned to an upright position and stood to go. *Right?*

"What would you do, Dad?" To his surprise, he'd said that aloud.

The only sound came from the coin on the desk, knocked sliding by his hand. He picked it up to study the inscription. "Faith. Honor. Integrity."

Geoff's phone went off in his pocket. Lost in thought, he ignored the ring.

"He can't rest until that happens," the girl had said.

When the phone beeped, he checked his voicemail, swinging side to side in the swivel chair. Katie's high-priority message asked him to come over that night before dinner. He listened, fiddling with the typewriter's carriage return. Paper inched up each time he pushed the lever.

Katie's voice went on, but Geoff had stopped paying attention. For there, on the document that had scrolled up from inside the ancient typewriter, **eight** words had neatly appeared:

I love you, son. Thank you for coming.

Chapter Twenty-Seven

AUGUST 3

Darby ran into Justin Tuesday morning at Branch Hall's stairway on her way to the Music Room. "Wish me luck. I'm rehearsing with the dancers."

"You'll be fine."

Crossing her fingers, she ran upstairs and peeked in the door where Maria was running drills with the chorus line, her head keeping time with the words. "Step, kick, step together..."

When the girls executed the choreography in something resembling synchronization, Darby could barely contain her relief. *They're not much better than I am.*

Maria readied the Karaoke track. "Try to project," she pleaded.

And Darby did. Her voice rang out, louder than it had ever been, while the dancers pirouetted frantically, most of them remaining on their feet.

"That was great!" applauded the counselors, and Monica slapped her a high five.

"Thanks." She dropped her head, too embarrassed to say more, much less credit Katie's poem for helping. After changing her shoes, she came face to face with Jessica, who asked, "What happened to you?"

"Yeah," said June. "I can practically hear you now," she added, a note of sarcasm in her tone.

Darby eyed the twins suspiciously, expecting a set up.

"I'm serious," Jessica insisted. "You've gotten so much better."

"Well," Darby responded carefully, "In a way, I have you to thank."

"For what?"

"If you hadn't, um, forced me to be in the Talent Show," she said with a sly expression, "I never would be able to get up on a stage in f-f-front of people. I didn't think I could. I never would've even t-t-tried."

"We'll take credit," smirked June to her sister, but Jessica waved her off.

"That's pretty cool," she said, giving Darby a hasty hug before June pulled her out the door.

As Darby headed out of Branch Hall, she hid a smile, convinced Mr. Usher's voice sounded quietly in her ear. "Keep going," it said. "All things are possible on Friday."

Friday. That's August sixth. Will Geoff change his mind? She crossed her fingers, and her wrists for extra luck.

Just then, someone called her name. *It's Katie... with her brothers.* Darby cringed, imagining for a second, they'd come to interrogate her about Mr. Usher.

But Katie greeted her like an old buddy. "We're on our way to meet with Donna," she explained, adding, "I don't think you've met my brothers."

Darby braced herself when she shook hands with Geoff.

"You look familiar, but I can't say we've been introduced," he said, slipping her a private wink.

She relaxed, her eyes aglow with amusement, "Nice to meet you *now.*"

Geoff laughed heartily.

They seem pretty happy. Are they here about the deal? Before she could ask, they headed inside.

~∞~

Geoff knocked on the camp director's half-open door.

"Come in!" Donna jumped up. "What news do you have?" she asked before they were seated. "Your phone message sounded very mysterious."

Geoff snapped open his briefcase, pulling out a legal folder. "We came up with an idea. Actually, it was Katie's."

She shook her head. "It was yours too."

"Well," he said, "Dad always did what was best for us. I'm just returning the favor. Anyway, we all hope we've found a way to get full-market value for Dad's property while putting it in your name."

Donna raised an eyebrow, glancing through his papers.

"We propose," Geoff continued, "that you purchase two-thirds of the property with the money you've offered. In exchange for the remaining third, Katie, Chad, and I would become minority partners. If you'll have us," he nodded, reacting to Donna's startled expression. "You could eventually buy us out, but it would mean a lot to stay involved with Dad's legacy."

"This is too…" Donna's voice choked. She covered her face with her hands, her shoulders shaking.

The siblings shared an uncomfortable glance. *"Doesn't she like the idea?"* Geoff mouthed.

But Donna regained her composure and dabbed her eyes with a tissue. "Well, now. I hope you don't object to an overly emotional business partner." She beamed. "Where do I sign?"

~ ⁊ ~

MIDNIGHT...

Late that night, Darby kicked off her blanket and tossed onto her side. The full moon cast silvery rays shining over her like a spotlight. She breathed deeply, a pleasant dream leaving a half smile on her face.

Occasional breezes rustled the leaves, but it was quiet otherwise, human inhabitants having fallen asleep at least an hour before. In the stillness, even hooting owls and other wildlife seemed to be slumbering. If by chance, amid such serenity, Darby had been sitting at one of the popsicle-colored cookout tables, she would certainly have noticed a bright flare in the trees. But with no one around when a giant swirling cylinder of fireflies whooshed out from the west, they headed for South Circle unobserved. When they arrived outside her window, their sheer mass threw a shadow through the glass.

Darby started awake, rapt at the spectacle of countless hovering lights flickering on and off like Morse code. In less than a minute, as if the fireflies had been part of her dream, their silent invitation rang loud and clear. She donned a T-shirt, jeans, and shoes and stole down the cabin steps, following as they swooped in the direction of North Circle.

The display repeated at Naz's window, then Justin's, sending both boys outside to meet up with her.

Naz pulled the paperweight from his pocket and held it up. "Surprise!" The orange circle was complete.

After Darby and the boys silently exchanged jubilant high fives, the three friends traveled toward summer's last adventure at Leroy Usher, Carnival King, full of anticipation.

Chapter Twenty-Eight

The night air outside the big orange building carried a promise of excitement within. Even the trolley, which brought them over the wall quickly, as if sensing Darby's impatience, flew colored flags from every pole. Calliope music, faraway laughter, and shouts from children's voices drew her into the warehouse, with Justin and Naz on her heels.

Mr. Usher stood polishing his watch in front of the archway of lights, where scores of circling rides, clanking games, and flashing signs awaited beyond.

"Look!" Darby handed him the paperweight, but the smile illuminating his face told her he already knew.

"I thank you all. Without you, it never would have happened." After shaking hands with each, he pocketed the paperweight along with his silent watch then beckoned them to follow. "Tonight, we simply celebrate."

As they passed Timeless Voyages, Naz asked if they could take its Journey to Mars, but Mr. Usher gestured at the crimson, amber, and cobalt streamers, which hung motionless behind a large, white sign. CLOSED FOR NOW, it said, nearly hidden in shadows. "Perhaps another summer. Now come along. Darby, where shall we begin?"

Without hesitating, she decided on the merry-go-round and climbed onto the scarlet-bridled white horse she rode during her first visit to L.U.C.K. As they circled the colorful, noisy carnival, she recalled the warehouse's dark, cluttered insides that day. *So different... like me.*

After the ride slowed, they ran toward River Caverns, Naz's choice, to board mini canoes that floated through narrow canals, every lane filled with water of different colors. Justin picked Sunset Safari Adventure complete with realistic elephants, lions, giraffes, and tigers. With stops in between for tastes of cotton candy, they swung through the air aboard Jets of the Future, explored an ocean on Undersea Octopus Dive, spun around the Tilt-A-Whirl, splashed through a Log Ride, and screamed themselves hoarse on the Ghost Train. Finally, Darby, Justin, and Naz took turns posing inside a curtained photo booth, the last camera clicks a group shot, their smiles bright as sunshine.

Mr. Usher met them outside the old machine to wait for their picture strips. He cleared his throat. "It's time for farewells."

"Right now?" Naz's mouth turned downward like an unhappy-face icon.

"Indeed. But life is full of many adventures to come."

"When I get home," he declared, "I'm going to tell Mamá how extraordinary you are, how exceptional, remarkable, outstanding…"

Mr. Usher chuckled when Naz stopped for breath. "You have learned your English well, which is a very impressive accomplishment."

Justin straightened his shoulders. "I'll never forget how you made it possible for me to say goodbye to my dad," he said.

"Keep him alive here," said Mr. Usher, pointing at Justin's heart, "and be sure to savor time with those who are still living."

When he turned to Darby, she shook her head and her eyes filled with tears. "I wish I could think of a way to thank you."

"All that you gave came back to benefit yourself." He offered his handkerchief. "It seems I was right all along about your intrepid, brave nature, yes?"

Before Darby had time to think of a reply, the camera machine delivered three strips into her hands, and she cackled with the boys about their silly expressions. Then she fell silent, spellbound by the group photo. In every picture, Mr. Usher stood behind them.

Darby turned to him, disbelieving, but he'd taken the boys into the foyer, so she followed. When she passed under the archway, the carnival fell still. A balloon burst. She turned back. Darkness now covered everything beyond.

Outside, Darby encircled Mr. Usher with a mammoth embrace. "Will we ever see you again?" she asked, returning his handkerchief.

"I think it's too soon to know," he replied, assisting her onto the trolley where the boys waited. "However," he added, "all things are possible."

The engines fired up, the kids waved goodbye, and the trolley lifted off.

As they sailed into the night sky, Darby watched Mr. Usher get smaller and smaller. Just before she lost sight of him, he removed his top hat and took a deep bow.

Chapter Twenty-Nine

AUGUST 6

The only time more chaotic than the first day of camp was the last, but even in the swirling sea of kids and parents on the Great Lawn, Justin easily found his mom. He hurried to greet her, emerging from an extended hug with flushed cheeks.

She brushed his hair back from his forehead. "It's been a long eight weeks," she said. "You've grown a bit... and you look even more like your father." She turned away to pull a tissue from her purse.

"Mom?" asked Justin, his throat tightening at the melancholy that clouded her eyes. *Now she'll change the subject.*

Instead, she simply blew her nose. "It took me a long time to be able to talk about your dad and how much I miss him," she said. "I'm sorry I made it so difficult for you, dear."

Somewhat speechless, Justin stared at the ground. Then his resolve to never again choose silence as a solution kicked in. "I'm okay, really. Let's go see my bird feeder. It won a First Prize ribbon in the Natural World category."

"How, um, lovely," she said. "What's it made of?"

"Oh, lots of stuff. Wire, twigs, string, and a little mud to hold it together. Don't worry, though, I won't bring it into the house. It's supposed to be kept outdoors."

"We can keep it in the shed, where I moved your popsicle collection."

"I thought you threw it away."

"Well, no. I decided to wait for you to get back so we could go through the house and make some decisions together."

A slow smile spread over his face. *This summer turned out better than anything I could have thought.*

Naz waited for Mamá's arrival, locked in a hotly contested game of War with Brough. "Ace, yes," he crowed, gathering the winning cards.

Rich poked his head in the door. "Someone's parents are here, and you guys are the last two Rangers. C'mon out."

"They must be yours," said Naz. "My Mamá is coming by herself."

Brough jumped up and ran to the porch but was back in a flash. "Nope, not mine. They're always late."

Naz scratched his cheek, laid down the cards, and walked outside. He froze, blinking hard, unsure whether he was imagining the olive-skinned man standing next to Mamá or not. But when the man held out his arms, Naz came back to life. "Papá!" he screamed, running into his father's embrace. "You are here! You are here!" He caught his breath, enfolding Mamá in an equally exuberant hug. "You are really here!"

"I could not miss your homecoming from camp or being with my family again." Papá took Mamá's hand. "We have much to discuss."

His eyes glistening, Naz led them to the picnic grounds, almost floating with joy.

$\sim$

After Darby and her parents picked up box lunches, she brought them to a turquoise picnic table. "Let's eat here. It's my friends' and my favorite spot."

"So tell us about camp," said Dad, while her mom pulled out some business charts. "Marcia." He sighed. "You can do that later."

"This last round of ad copy is due Monday," Mom insisted. "I need to perfect it."

Darby smiled inwardly at something Mr. Usher had taught her. *Perhaps your mother judges herself too harshly…* "M-m-mom," she began. The familiar frown that broke across her mother's face breezed past without leaving a mark. "I bet if you worked as hard as you usually do, it's probably f-f-fine just like it is."

At first, her mom didn't move, as if her eyes had gotten stuck on her chart, and Darby thought maybe she hadn't heard. But when Mom raised her head, the frown had vanished. She met Darby's gaze. Her mouth opened as if to speak, then she held up her hands in mock surrender. "Has your father been coaching you?"

Struck silent with surprise, Darby shook her head.

"You heard your dad," said Mom, storing her chart in her purse. "Tell us about camp. Sounds like you've enjoyed your summer."

Darby's voice returned, as though chatting with her mom was the most familiar thing in the world. "You w-w-wouldn't believe how much." Without even mentioning L.U.C.K., she had plenty to tell them.

At two o'clock, families and staff overflowed the picnic tables, and the Talent Show got underway.

Darby and her cabin mates, last to perform, watched from seats near the stage. During the Charging Buffaloes joke skit, she laughed loudest for Justin's straight-man act, especially when he asked, "What do mountains talk about?" and his friend Eugene deadpanned, "Oh, a range of topics." By the time Rich's Rangers were demonstrating their bird calls, she was on her way to the costume tent, but she cheered along with the families when Naz, without missing a syllable, announced, "Budgerigar parakeet."

As it came time to go on, Darby stared at the audience from

around the side of the stage.

"Just one more group's ahead of us," said Maria, touching up Darby's curls.

"I didn't think there'd be so many people. Do I l-l-look okay?" she asked, but Maria was already busy lining up the Wild Strawberries dancers for their entrance.

With no one else to talk to, Darby pulled at the hem of her skirt. She reeled off Katie's poem for the third time that day. Then she scanned the crowd, silently conveying *Hi* to Justin. He turned her way and sent back a thumbs up that filled her with hope.

"And now," broadcast a voice from the speakers, "please welcome Darby McAllister and the Wild Strawberries."

Darby walked up the stairs onto the stage, her stomach fluttering. She found her mark in front of the chorus line, closed her eyes for a second, and soaked up the sun's warmth. The spectators quieted down. The music launched its intro. She counted down to her cue.

Now! Darby began singing, her voice steady and strong.

In a flash, it was over. Amid the applauding crowd, she saw her mom leap to her feet, her arms waving in tribute. Darby choked up with euphoric tears and stepped back into the chorus line for a group bow.

I pulled it off! Seized by the urge to turn a cartwheel, as if she had ever even attempted such a feat, she resisted, but her face glowed as she followed the dancers off.

Mr. Usher had called her intrepid and brave. Now she believed it herself, and she sent him silent thanks. *Wherever he is.*

Backstage, Monica, Naz, Justin, Lindsay, other cabin mates, and even people she didn't know, surrounded her with congratulations. Mom and Dad made their way through the crowd to wrap her in a bear hug, and when her father hoisted her in the air, she screamed in delight.

Later, while parents waited outside Branch Hall for luggage, Darby ran inside to catch a few last moments with Naz and Justin. Almost immediately, she stopped short.

Ahead of them, the Usher family portrait had been mounted on the back wall. Mr. Usher's likeness filled the formerly empty place on the canvas.

"He's finally back with his wife," she said.

"That's why it looked off balance before," chuckled Justin.

Naz nodded. "He's at rest."

"Exactly where he should be," said an adult voice behind them. "Right?"

They spun around. Geoff stood beside his brother and sister.

"Right," replied Darby. "Why is it here?"

"So he'll be around kids," said Katie, "no matter how long he's been gone."

They all shared a quiet laugh.

Before the siblings left for Donna's office, Katie turned back to Darby. "Quite a performance!" she said, tilting her head toward her father's likeness. "He would be very proud."

Darby grinned, touching her pendant. She and her pals dawdled in front of the painting as long as they could before heading down Branch Hall's steps and over to the parking area.

When they got to her dad's SUV, Darby threw her arms over the boys' shoulders, trying not to count how many months stood between now and the start of camp next year. "I guess we won't see each other for a while."

"Maybe time will go quicker than we think," said Justin.

Naz agreed.

She sighed. "I hope so."

They shared a final hug, and Justin helped her into the back. As her dad drove out to White Falls Highway, Darby rolled down the window. She waved to the boys until she could no longer see them. Then she stretched out on the seat, brimming with indelible memories of a summer almost too amazing to be true.

Almost.

TO BE CONTINUED NEXT SUMMER...

Acknowledgments

Summer of L.U.C.K.'s road to the present day has been lengthy and circuitous, and to have "the book of my heart" now published is a dream come true. Thank you to Jana Grissom and Kaylee Grissom at INtense Publications for making that possible.

I'd like to acknowledge Frank Weimann, David Lasley, and Dan Smetanka for their contributions early on in the journey.

Big thanks are due to my friends Libby Huebner, Ella Johnson, Lynne Heffley, and my sister, Susan Segal, who have been along for the ride since the very beginning. And to Kitty Felde for inspiring me to think outside the box. I also send deepest appreciation for their enthusiasm and encouragement to my friends who Beta read over the years, especially Beth Miller, Tamikka Forbes, Danielle Aubuchon Blocker, Sabrina Skacan, Megan Hilliard, Denise Abbott-Shoemaker, Eleni Ford, Eve Gleichman and Laura Webb Zachar.

The kids in the literacy program at Marylhurst School in West Linn, Oregon, their teacher Mary Mahorney, and Ann Brown, who connected me with them, will never know how much their input meant to me.

I also send a shoutout to Brenda Drake, whose support for fellow writers introduced me to the online writers community, which changed everything; to mega-agent Janet Reid, who so tirelessly supports writers she doesn't even know; and to Jessi Cole Jackson, an early critique partner.

My love and thanks must also be sent to Cori

Newlander, Lisa Sanchez, Monica Joynes, and all my fellows who have lifted me up and given me solutions for many years. I am truly blessed to know you all.

But the person whose contributions to *Summer of L.U.C.K.* have been greatest is my steadfast critique partner (and friend) Leila Rheaume. From across the country, she provided guidance, feedback and input that changed the story's direction. As she gave so generously of her time (and patience), I became a better writer. Above all, Leila believed in *Summer of L.U.C.K.* and helped me stay intrepid despite the rejection that all writers face. Thank you forever.

And finally, I thank God, and I thank my husband and family, to whom this book is lovingly dedicated.

To *Summer of L.U.C.K.* readers:

If you enjoyed the adventures of Darby, Justin and Naz, keep an eye out for its sequel, *Summer of L.U.C.K.: Ready or Not*, which INtense Publishing will publish in 2021. There is no greater support you can give a debut author than your word-of-mouth-recommendation, so I hope you'll consider posting a review on Amazon, Goodreads, or other places.

Please feel free to sign up for my mailing list at laurastegman.com and follow me: Twitter @LauraStegman and Instagram @laura_stegman

About the Author:

Laura Segal Stegman grew up in Southern California with parents who valued reading, and she remains spellbound by middle grade fiction. Some of her favorites, then and now, are *The Diamond in the Window*, *Ellen Tebbits*, *All of A Kind Family*, *Wonder*, *A Patron Saint for Junior Bridesmaids*, *Harry Potter and the Sorcerer's Stone* and *The Miraculous*. As a writer, Laura's non-fiction credits include collaboration on the travel book *Only in New York*, and her feature stories have appeared in the *Los Angeles Times*, *Los Angeles Magazine*, *Westways Magazine* and *Christian Science Monitor,* among others. A long-time publicist, she owns Laura Segal Stegman Public Relations, LLC, which has represented a wide-ranging client list of businesses, arts organizations and non-profit events over the years. She is a Phi Beta Kappa graduate of UC Irvine with a B.A. in Drama and lives with her husband in West Los Angeles and part-time in New York City. She loves reading, L.A. Dodgers baseball, classical music and theater. *Summer of L.U.C.K.* is her debut novel.

Visit Laura at: www.laurastegman.com Twitter: @LauraStegman Instagram: @laura_stegman Facebook: www.facebook.com/LauraSegalStegmanAuthor/

Continue reading for a sneak peek into Book 2 by Laura
Segal Stegman:

Summer of
L.U.C.K.:

Ready or Not

Chapter One

JUNE 13

In all his thirteen years, Justin Pennington had never been good with surprises. Not that it was much of a revelation to find out that life was unfair. The real shock had come last month, when he caught on just how *totally* unfair. Still, he arrived at Camp Inch confident L.U.C.K.'s magic would make things right, exactly like it had last summer.

Moments after Mom steered her SUV into the only empty spot in the camp's parking area, Justin threw open the door and sprang out, scanning the swarming crowds. Before he knew it, his official cabin assignment envelope had arrived and guys in STAFF T-shirts were loading his footlocker into one of a dozen pick-up trucks circling the asphalt. The search for Darby would have to wait.

Prying himself from Mom's goodbye hug as fast as he could, he grabbed his duffel bag and hopped into a nearby electric camper transport cart. As Mom waved, the driver rolled off to pick up other kids.

Justin twisted around. "When you get home," he hollered at his mom, "don't forget to check with Naz's parents to see how he's doing."

The driver collected a bunch of chattering girls who seemed almost as excited as Justin. He settled back and toasted his smiling face in the sun, its warmth tempered by a slight breeze that wove through the tall trees. Nine months of counting down until camp started again were over.

Although he expected things to be different this year, he wasn't sure just how different. Camp Inch's expansion, announced in a "Welcome Back" packet mailed with forms and instructions for his second summer here, was old news. But aside from plenty more campers lounging on the porch of Branch Hall, the big white building where meals were served, everything looked the same. So far.

Justin scrambled to his feet, ready to jump out as the cart approached the plaza in front of South Circle and North Circle where all the cabins were located last summer. When the driver kept going, he almost yelled, "Stop!" Checking his cabin assignment envelope, he squinted in confusion. Stamped on the front in big letters under the SUMMER 2000 date was OAK LOOP, followed by #16, written in ink. Justin's fingers tightened on the cart railing. *Oak what?*

The cart drove on, winding past grassy patches and beds of flowers in rainbow colors. Soon he got his first clue about changes. On land which he guessed had been last year's picnic grounds and ball field stood two new cabin circles. *Or cabin loops*, he thought, making a face. *Everything in camp has a goofy name. They should have called them Froot Loops.*

Right when it occurred to him to wonder if they'd still have cookouts and where they'd play ball games, the driver pulled up at a tree-ringed plaza. It seemed an exact match for the one fronting South and North Circles, except for its signs. While the girls ran off to Pine Loop, Justin hesitated before heading into Oak Loop. *If Darby's still in South Circle, we're kind of far from each other. And who knows where they'll put Naz when he gets here. If he does.*

Once he entered, the forest green roofs on Oak Loop's wood cabins, exactly like those in North Circle, put him at ease. Even better, he spotted Eugene, his bunkmate from last year, among the kids on the steps of what presumably was #16. His smile returned.

Eugene ran toward him with a wave. "Hey, it's about time."

"My mom forgot about how far away we live from this part of Michigan. I thought we'd never get here."

Heaving the duffel onto his shoulder, Eugene nearly fell backwards until Justin helped steady him. He towed Justin up the stairs into a cabin almost exactly like last summer's. "I know you wanted a window, but this bunk bed by the door was the only one left when I got here."

Justin counted five twin bunks, several with campers

unloading their stuff. *That's one less than last year.* He'd already heard that counselors slept somewhere else when you turn thirteen or older, but this settled it. So with or without a window for Darby to tap on, he'd have no problem sneaking out to meet her and Naz for midnight visits to L.U.C.K. "Doesn't matter. Thanks for saving me a top bunk."

Eugene wasn't any taller than last year, and as he dusted their bedframe with a wet wipe, Justin grinned. *He hasn't changed at all.* Some of the guys last summer mocked him as "Eugene the Clean," but Justin had grown almost as close to him as he had to his best friends Darby and Naz. He and Eugene had talked a few times since camp ended, reliving their hit comedy act at camp's Talent Show and thinking up ideas for this year.

As Eugene informed him they were the only two Charging Buffalos in Oak Loop, they swung Justin's duffel onto the top bunk. "I saw a couple of the other guys from last year, but they're in North Circle. Now that camp's gotten bigger, there's two cabins for us thirteen-year-olds. But don't worry, I already met everyone here." He indicated the bunk at a right angle to theirs, one of two with a window. "Guys, this is Justin. That's Ronald." He pointed at a beefy kid, stockier than Justin, then at a blond, lanky boy. "And Sandy's up there."

While Justin nodded to both and climbed up the ladder to his bunk, Eugene ran outside, calling, "I'll be right back."

"He thinks he's our social director, introducing everyone." Ronald snickered, looking up at his bunkmate. "Sandy. Isn't that a girl's name?"

The blond kid shrugged. "It can be. But it's for guys too. I'm named after Koufax."

"Seriously?" Justin, who loved baseball more than ice cream, leaned across and slapped Sandy a high five.

"Who's that?" Ronald's laugh sounded like a bark. "Your ancient great-grandmother?"

Justin snorted. "Are you for real? Sandy Koufax is only one of the greatest pitchers ever. The youngest player ever elected to the Hall of Fame, four no hitters, a perfect–"

Ronald cut him off with, "Not interested," and turned his attention to a kid on his other side.

"Baseball must not be his thing," said Sandy with a grin that revealed a mouth full of metal braces. "My dad works for the Dodgers, so it's sure mine."

Justin's eyebrows shot up, as if Sandy had revealed that Koufax, the fabled 1960s Dodger player, planned to come out of retirement. His own favorite team was the hometown Milwaukee Brewers, but the Los Angeles club was a close second, especially since the Brewers' manager this season happened to be a former Dodger. After Sandy set his head spinning with tales of catch with players and clubhouse visits,

Justin asked, "Why would you pick camp over that?"

"My dad's scouting all over the country this summer, and my mom's with some Michigan relatives, so I'm here."

Eugene stuck his head inside to summon them out for popsicles, and they both whooped as they slid down.

"Hey, Sandy Kojak, use the ladder," Ronald grumbled. "You better not wake me up at night shaking the bed like that."

"My last name's not Kojak, or even Koufax. It's Steinfeld."

"Seinfeld? Like that Jew boy on TV?" Rather than asking a real question, Ronald's tone contained a challenge.

Justin shuddered as if he'd tasted something disgusting. "Jew boy" was on a list of "Bigoted Expressions" he remembered from his class visit to Milwaukee's Tolerance Center.

Sandy, who looked like he was trying to decide whether Ronald was stupid or just being a jerk, said nothing. But neither did Justin. Just like he'd kept his mouth closed when some kids yelled at Naz about his olive-colored skin. At first, he thought his friend hadn't heard, but right after, Naz's bike skidded on some hosed off sidewalk, and he broke his arm.

The nasty words had made Justin's stomach churn then, like Ronald's slur did now. *So why don't I tell him to shut up?* It wasn't like when Justin stayed silent for months after his dad died. This was different. *This was because of what happened last month.*

To Justin's surprise, Eugene strode up to Ronald. "What difference does it make what religion anyone is?"

Justin held his breath.

Ronald glowered back. Then, without replying, he returned to his other conversation.

"C'mon." Eugene shook his head at Sandy and Justin. "Let's go meet some of the other guys." Outside, he introduced them to Counselors Brett and Ian and a group of boys kicking around a soccer ball.

While Justin got to know his new cabin mates over the next few hours, he kept his eye on Eugene to see if he would tell the counselors about Ronald's remark. The guides at the Tolerance Center made a big point of encouraging students to talk to an adult if someone harassed another kid.

And that's exactly what happened last month. After a teenager named Mitch punched a boy in the neighborhood park, Justin reported him to the security guard, proud of himself for doing the right thing. Like Luke Skywalker. And James Bond. But things hadn't worked out the way he'd expected. Not long after Mitch had been summoned to the park office, he'd shown up at the baseball diamond where Justin was practicing bat swings. Hissing, "Snitch," Mitch knocked him down with a punch to the stomach and ran off laughing, leaving Justin rolling on the infield grass. Though the pain had eventually faded, the ache of unfairness had not. That's when he remembered, as if he'd been punched again, that the good guys don't always win.

When the counselors summoned everyone for the opening cookout dinner, Ronald sauntered out, fake boxing with two other guys, ignoring Sandy, Justin, and Eugene as he walked by. Justin stared after him, his skin prickling like when Mitch had knocked him onto the grass. *Last summer Darby had some mean girls in her cabin. Now it's my turn.*

The trek to dinner took longer than it had last year, but Justin's rumbling stomach distracted him. Aromas from barbecue grills announced their presence long before the cabin mates arrived at the new cookout area, already teeming with campers. *It's huge.* He bobbed his head in approval. *Even bigger than last years.*

While Brett and Ian sorted the cabin mates into lines, Justin surveyed the grills, sizzling with hot dogs, chicken wings and burgers. Nearby, a buffet overflowed with potato salad, veggies, coleslaw, baked beans, fruit, and Camp Inch's signature lime-green Jell-O. He piled his plate with some of everything, went over to the brightly colored picnic tables so familiar from last year, took the seat Eugene had held for him, and dug into his food. Right before he started off for dessert, a tangle of reddish-brown curls in a group of passing girls caught his attention.

Darby! To avoid a repeat of the messy crash of baked beans and Jell-O that had introduced her to Naz and him last summer, he decided against dessert and dashed off, yelling her name.

She spun around, lighting up as she ran to greet him. "Finally!"

"How're you doing? How did that horse thing go?"

"It was a hard competition, but I won."

With a laugh, he made a "Duh" face.

"What about your baseball team, did you get to pitch in the finals?"

They caught up for a few minutes but when Justin brought up Naz's accident, a wave of dismay ran across her face. "I already heard. Is it true he's not coming to camp at all?"

"He's coming, but I'm not sure when. How did you know?"

"He left a voice mail at our house yesterday."

"My mom's checking how he's doing when she gets home." Justin tugged at his hair. "But I won't get her message from the camp office until tomorrow, so we..."

Before he could finish, a voice, almost inaudible, and seemingly from around the corner or perhaps from the trees across the path, sounded inside his head: *Our L.U.C.K. visits won't happen unless Naz is here, right?*

Justin didn't need to look around to see where the voice originated. He knew Darby had sent her thought *at* him using the magic that L.U.C.K. himself – Leroy Usher, Carnival King –

had bestowed on the three friends last summer. Somewhat breathless, he replied, "Right."

With a glimmer in her eye, she bent toward him, her relief matching his. "At least we can still understand each other without talking," she whispered.

Justin nodded, his head bursting with memories of Mr. Usher, their ghostly friend. The "Carnival King" nickname came from the amusement park rides and games he'd built in his orange warehouse on the property next to camp. From its dusty, gray jumble of crates and parts, it came alive as a real carnival under Mr. Usher's magical direction. Justin, Darby, and Naz never figured out how he did his magic, but last year, he'd sent his flying trolley late at night to bring them to the warehouse. From the first week of camp until they went home, he'd guided them through life-changing adventures on his Timeless Voyages ride. And they'd convinced his sons and daughter to merge the property with Camp Inch, granting his wish. But Mr. Usher's magic had conditions. If one of the trios was absent, things ground to a halt.

So, with Naz still home in Milwaukee, how could it be working now? Justin froze, breathing out a whistle. *What if he isn't home anymore?* Staring straight ahead, as if he'd find an answer in the nearby grove of trees, he caught Darby's eye and thought at her. *If the magic is working, Naz has to be somewhere nearby.*

Darby clapped her hand over her open mouth, as if she were about to explode with a scream. *Let's find out.*

Naz, where are you right now?

While they waited, Darby flapped her palms in front of her, as if that would mute the laughter and shouts from the kids surrounding them.

Ten seconds passed. It seemed like an hour. And then, ever so faintly, Justin caught two words.

I'm coming.

He released the breath he was holding.

"Did you hear that?" Darby's shriek attracted the attention of some nearby campers.

"Hear what?" said one.

"Um, n-n-nothing." She gave the kid a weak smile.

As Justin grabbed her arm, moving away to the relative privacy of the trees, he noticed that Darby no longer blushed when she stuttered. Thanks to Mr. Usher.

Almost there.

"That was Naz, for sure." Justin threw his fist into the air.

Darby shook her head. "We'll never find him in this crowd. He'll be coming from the cabins. Let's head there."

Justin, on his tiptoes, craned his neck. "There are two sets this year, and we don't know which one he's assigned to. I'm in a place called Oak Loop. Are you still in South Circle?"

"Yeah. No wonder this cookout place seemed farther away than last time."

Leading Darby back toward the picnic tables, Justin climbed up onto a bench. "All I see is my counselor getting ready to head out. Maybe I better…" Seconds later, the sight of a bright plaster cast sticking out from a black sling sped up his pulse. "There he is, looking for us. Hey!"

Darby joined him, waving.

They rushed toward Naz, breathless with excitement.

"You m-m-made it!" Darby threw her arms around him.

Even though her hug made Naz wince, his grin seemed undiminished. "Better late than never."

Justin played it safe and simply pointed to the cast. "You're okay?"

"I have a…" Naz took a folded piece of paper from inside the sling, fumbling to open it. "A hairline fracture," he read.

"How long do you have to wear that?"

"Five weeks."

"Wow, no swimming or…" Justin halted when Darby elbowed him, but not before Naz's face fell.

"It'll go fast." Darby leaned over to pat Naz. "And there will be three more weeks of camp after you get it taken off. We're just so glad you're here."

Naz brightened. "Moi aussi... me too." He pointed to Darby's head. "Your shorter coiffure looks quite excellent."

Justin held back a smile. Naz started learning English last summer when he and his mom came to the U.S. from their home in Morocco, and his word choices occasionally took an awkward turn.

Darby ran her hand from the top of Naz's head to hers. "You're practically as tall as I am." Turning to Justin, she added, "You're taller too."

"Took you long enough to notice."

"Well, you guys are lucky you live close enough to see each other any time, not just at Christmas break or here."

"Justin!" Eugene signaled from across the tables. "We're heading back to the cabin."

"I gotta go." Justin turned to Naz. "Where's your cabin?"

"North Circle." Naz pulled a felt marker from his pocket, handing it to Darby. "Before you depart, sign my cast." He pointed to a big empty rectangle among the signatures, happy face symbols, and musical notes. "I reserved this for you two."

After Justin eyed the miniscule area left by the gigantic "Darby McAllister," he scrawled his name, trying not to mess up her handiwork. Meanwhile a man whose deep suntan made his bushy hair look even lighter told Naz to come get some dinner before the food was gone.

The trio agreed to meet up at breakfast, and Justin ran to catch his cabin mates. As they trekked back to Oak Loop under a star-filled sky, he remembered that the bushy-haired man was Woody, Naz's counselor last summer. Years back, when L.U.C.K.'s Ferris wheel and tilt-a-whirl rides were open to Camp Inch kids, Woody had been a camper.

Justin pictured Mr. Usher's blue eyes, their twinkle so reassuring, the big top hat perched on his wavy black hair, his cropped red jacket sporting big gold buttons, and the ivory pants tucked into tall black boots. He rested in peace now, but when they asked if they'd ever see him again, he'd boomed, "All things are possible." Justin heard that as a "yes." In fact, he counted on it.

After he and his cabin mates piled inside and dressed for bed, Counselor Brett asked for group name suggestions.

"Charging Buffalos," snickered Justin to Eugene, who looked up from the shoe he was polishing.

"That was our name last year."

Justin dropped his head backward. "Joke."

Eugene cracked a sheepish grin.

"Sir?"

Justin bent over, surprised at the respectful voice coming from the lower bunk next to his.

When the counselor replied in a similar manner, saying,

"Call me Brett, young man," Justin wondered which of them was faking out the other. It had to be the mean kid, who had never been anything but unpleasant.

"How about Mutant Crusaders?"

"No way! Mutants are gross." Justin shook his head, but a couple of other boys hooted their approval and the counselor offered Ronald a thumbs up. *And was that a dirty look Brett just aimed at me? For what?*

"Great, we're set. Thanks, Ronald."

"Okay, Mutants," added Counselor Ian, while Justin groaned into his pillow, "let's get ready to turn in so we can get up early to try out the new carnival."

At first Justin wondered if Ian had maybe said, "Carvel," the ice cream place, not carnival. Or could it be that he'd actually be returning to the Leroy Usher, Carnival King, warehouse in less than 24 hours? He had to know. "What new carnival?" He meant his voice to sound casual, but somehow it rose, like a girl's.

"I guess not everyone knows about this," said Ian, "It's a new part of Camp Inch this year, with rides like in an outdoor carnival, only inside."

While the other guys buzzed eagerly, Justin slam-dunked his t-shirt into the laundry basket Eugene had set up for them. "Yeah!" Then he thought at Darby and Naz: *Are your cabins going to L.U.C.K. tomorrow too?* Silence drifted back. *It can't be that this loopy cabin is too far from South and North Circle.* Mr. Usher's magic didn't transmit every thought, only those they wanted to share. *Like this one. So maybe they're just asleep.*

Justin settled underneath the covers, his thoughts tumbling over each other at the prospect of visiting the warehouse. *Will Mr. Usher's office look the same? What rides will be left?* The architectural drawings in his registration packet hadn't said much, describing it only as an added play area. Even so, the pages grew tattered after he and Naz had searched them endlessly for clues during one of their visits last spring. He tossed onto one side, then the other.

Finally, long after the counselors were gone, he lay still, drifting toward sleep... until something super cold under the blanket touched his foot that absolutely, positively did not belong there. Justin bolted upright, almost blurting out a swear word. He grabbed his flashlight, dove back under, and aimed it at the intruder: a small metallic orange box. He nudged it with his finger, every muscle tensing as he imagined a bony claw busting out and grabbing him. But it just sat there.

His pounding heart slowed. Placing the box in his palm, he flicked open the hinged lid, an involuntary twitch jerking his head backwards. Nothing flew out, so he bent forward. Inside lay a smaller box, also orange, with a glossy silver seal that held fast when he attempted to break it. He ran his fingers over some embossed printing on the top, too tiny to see in the dim light, but he managed to make out a Y. Then an A... D... and G. *YADG? What does that mean?* When he turned it over, though, he smiled at four large letters. They spelled "L.U.C.K."

After twisting onto his back, he lowered the blanket from his face to see if anyone else had been surprised by something in their bedding. The other guys lay still.

In another attempt to reach Darby and Naz, he squeezed his eyes shut. *Did you get anything from Mr. Usher? Are you going to the warehouse?* When his questions went unanswered yet again, he tossed off the blanket in frustration, almost losing the orange box over the side.

Justin clutched it to his chest, his eyes falling on Ronald's lumpy shape one bunk over, almost as ugly as his words had been this afternoon. Above him in the top bunk, Sandy's fair hair shone in moonlight coming through the window.

Not for the first time, Justin chewed himself out for not coming to Sandy's defense. Last summer, he'd resolved to never again choose silence as a solution. *If Dad was alive, he would say I should have spoken up, like Eugene did.* An itchy flush crawled up his neck as he worried he'd never get over the memory of Mitch's fist in his gut. *I'm better than that. I want to be better than that.*

When he opened his fingers, the orange box in his palm reminded him that Mr. Usher – and his magical powers – still lived. Slipping it deep inside his pillowcase for safekeeping, he began drifting off with a sigh of relief. And just before he withdrew his hand, the little box grew warm.

CPSIA information can be obtained
at www.ICGtesting.com
Printed in the USA
FSHW020609230820
73188FS